SAN CARLOS HORSE SOLDIER

When renegade Apache Joe escapes the hangman, Limm Sieber, the bounty hunter who had captured him, vows to bring Joe back to justice. But the renegade is on a cattle drive to Montana. Sieber joins the drive along the hazardous Bozeman Trail where, ironically, both men are forced to fight side by side. Each knows that a showdown between them cannot be avoided once they reach Montana — but overshadowing them is the fearful knowledge that death is about to strike.

Books by Terry Murphy
in the Linford Western Library:

HE RODE WITH QUANTRILL
CANYON OF CROOKED SHADOWS

TERRY MURPHY

SAN CARLOS HORSE SOLDIER

Complete and Unabridged

LINFORD
Leicester

First published in Great Britain in 1997 by
Robert Hale Limited
London

First Linford Edition
published 1998
by arrangement with
Robert Hale Limited
London

The right of Terry Murphy to be identified
as the author of this work has been asserted
by her in accordance with the
Copyright, Designs and Patents Act, 1988

British Library CIP Data

Murphy, Terry, *1962–*
San Carlos horse soldier.—Large print ed.—
Linford western library
1. Western stories
2. Large type books
I. Title
823.9'14 [F]

ISBN 0–7089–5366–2

Published by
F. A. Thorpe (Publishing) Ltd.
Anstey, Leicestershire

Set by Words & Graphics Ltd.
Anstey, Leicestershire
Printed and bound in Great Britain by
T. J. International Ltd., Padstow, Cornwall

This book is printed on acid-free paper

1

Apache Joe was due to be hanged at four o'clock that afternoon. At noon, Sheriff Phil Comber had a knotted-up pain in his gut and a steadily increasing ache in his head. Life had suddenly become terribly unfair. There hadn't been a hanging in the county for more than three decades. At that time he had been deputy to old Hank Griswald, and had been able to turn his head away at the crucial, horrifying moment. Even so, the face of the condemned man, a Mexican who had knifed to death his wife and her lover, had haunted Comber's days and nights ever since. He would have preferred it had the Mexican showed signs of distress, or even resisted as he was taken to the gallows, but he had walked beside Sheriff Griswald like the pair of them were off to take a drink together. Luck had saved Phil Comber from having to conduct an execution during his thirty years as sheriff. But now, with less than twelve months to go to his retirement, his good fortune had ended. How would Apache Joe react when the time came for the noose to be dropped over his black-haired head? What should have been the tranquil twilight of Comber's career had been shattered the day bounty hunter Limm Sieber had ridden into town leading a horse on which a sullen Apache Joe sat, trussed as securely as a turkey ready for Thanksgiving.

Apache Joe was a mystery, the only sure thing about him being the handbill that had been circulated offering a reward for his capture. It was all legal and above-board, otherwise Sieber, a hard man of very few words, would not have been involved. The renegade was tried and sentenced to death by the travelling judge, and now the grim, final chapter of the story was Comber's responsibility.

In the opinion of the sheriff, Apache Joe was no worse nor better than any of the wild young men who roamed that untamed land. He had been a highly respected sergeant in the Apache government scouts until leaving the reservation at San Carlos to track down and kill the two white men who had raped and murdered his sister. Had the law assessed the situation sensibly and logically, then Joe would have been congratulated, shaken by the hand, and reinstated as a scout. But they had declared him to be an outlaw, leaving him no option but to act like one. With his band of five young Apaches who had absconded from the agency at San Carlos to be with him, Apache Joe had rustled cattle and horses, robbed wagon-trains, and had kidnapped women, both Indian and whites, abandoning them in the desert when they no longer interested him. In doing these things he had murdered any man foolish enough to attempt to stop him.

There was a fast-growing belief that Joe was not an Apache. It was said that he wasn't even a 'breed, as not one drop of Indian blood pulsed through his veins. It was, those who claimed to know said, just the extreme length of his jet-black hair that fooled people into thinking he was an Apache.

Whether or not this was true Comber didn't know, and was too perplexed to care. Apache Joe had been a quiet, model prisoner, which was something to be thankful for. Lithe and handsome, Joe had an air of unconcern, but the perceptive Comber recognized this as cultivated, for it was betrayed by the constant alertness in the prisoner's dark eyes. He hadn't even taken advantage of Arthur Greening, a boy deputy who would be a pushover for a man like Apache Joe.

All of the troubles, the complications that were blighting the life of Sheriff Phil Comber, had come not from inside but from outside the jail. They had begun with the arrival of a portly young gentleman with a ruddy, cheerful visage, who had conversationally announced that he was the official hangman assigned the task of building a scaffold and executing Apache Joe.

'I am a perfectionist, an artist, Sheriff,' the man, who was balding but couldn't have been much past thirty years of age, had said enthusiastically, when enquiring if there were a couple of reliable local carpenters he could employ. 'I am an authority in the science of inflicting death by means of the halter. The bad old days of the 'trap gallows' have gone forever, Sheriff, and jolly good riddance.'

Giving his name only as William, he had started work immediately, supervising two men on the building of a gallows with the total dedication and precision of someone charged with the construction of a grand palace for an emperor. William was an affable enough young fellow, and his keenness couldn't be faulted, but Comber was ill at ease when close to this man who had devoted his life to ending the lives of others.

Yet there were plenty in town who didn't share the sheriff's revulsion. Each evening they readily bought drinks for William so they could sit, completely fascinated, listening to William say how, as a simple cabinet maker, his life had been changed by reading the autobiography of Jack Ketch, the renowned high-executioner of Great Britain.

'I studied hard in every spare hour available to me,' William would say again and again for different audiences, reminiscence of tough times moistening his eyes each time. 'I visited the slaughter-house to familiarize myself with the windlass used for hoisting animals. I did this with a view to applying the same principles for the humane accommodation of the law-breaking community.'

Over the days, Comber had adjusted to having the eccentric hangman around town. In a way it was a relief, for William could, and no doubt eagerly would, take much of the unpleasantness of executing a man from the sheriff.

But that morning had brought further complications with another new arrival. Putting a dainty ankle on display as she stepped down from the morning stage, came a petite woman whose stunning beauty was projected by a mass of flowing, glowing red hair. Apparently unaware of, or most probably accustomed to the stir her presence was causing, she looked around her, spotted the sheriff's office, picked up her well-worn, heavy valise, and did a head-high march to the jail.

Just as if this was an everyday occurrence, she had introduced herself to Comber as Kitty McGlory, before going on to announce that she was there to marry Apache Joe. Taken aback by this, unable really to grasp that such a ludicrous situation had actually arisen, Comber's only response had been to rudely rush her out of his office back into the street.

The beautiful redhead had sought help and found it in the bulky person of the Reverend Lionel Anthom, a man whose face reddened and sweated greasily like the head of a roasting pig. Given to spouting poetry of his own invention, all of it orientated to the abhorrence of sin and lawlessness, Anthom had accompanied the woman back to the jailhouse, a fat arm comfortingly and protectively round her slim shoulder, startling her with his booming voice as he stepped into Comber's office.

Looking around the jail, disgust at having to enter such a den of iniquity purpling his heavy face, Anthom cried out, 'And then, too, the scrapes of seductions and rapes; and the foulest of crimes in the foulest of shapes. You are in a dreadful line of business, Sheriff Comber.'

'To each his own, Preacher,' Comber had managed to say before Anthom, supported by Kitty McGlory, was demanding to see Apache Joe.

When they were in the cage, the sheriff witnessed his first ever glimpse of animation in Apache Joe. The prisoner had stood up to embrace the redhead as Anthom had looked on, smiling fondly.

Anthom had expressed his willingness to perform the wedding ceremony, but Comber had objected, pointing out, 'Would you make this woman a wife in the knowledge that she'll be a widow two hours later, Preacher?'

'I would, and gladly so,' Anthom had nodded vigorously, spraying sweat with such force that the sheriff had needed to take a step backwards to avoid being showered. 'It must be God's will or this lady would not have been brought here to marry this man.'

A worried Comber had lost the argument, and he was anxious now by the sight of the woman, the preacher, and Justice Spencer heading for the jail, determination on the faces of all three. Kitty McGlory, who had an abrasiveness just below the surface of her undoubted beauty, did not strike the sheriff as a woman seeking some kind of emotional reward by marrying a man an hour or two before he was executed. As for Apache Joe, who by all accounts had known many women, he didn't appear to Comber as a man desirous of carrying an earthly ceremony over into the next world in the hope of some spiritual gain.

There was something very wrong, but Phil Comber couldn't put his finger on it. He was glad to see Justice Spencer coming to perform the civil part of the ceremony, for his presence relieved the sheriff of the onus of permitting the marriage to take place. But then Comber saw William come up behind the trio to slip into the office with them.

'What are you doing here, William?' Comber challenged the specialist hangman.

Leaning close, William nudged the

10

sheriff with an elbow and said in a conspiratorial whisper, 'I need to take another close look at my client — check the weight and height again, that sort of thing.'

'Very wise, very wise,' the Reverend Anthom intoned. 'Because of the absence of a caring man like William, Sheriff Comber, the visitation of death upon Angelo Cornetti in New York was most horrifying.'

William bobbed his head in vehement agreement. 'Indeed, indeed. Didn't we read that 'his terrorized clamour was like the barking of a dog as he was led to the scaffold, and his body was not sufficiently heavy to produce the requisite rebound to dislocate the neck, so that death came through strangulation in a way that sickened all onlookers'? I take a genuine pride in my work, Sheriff Comber, I am not merely the man who cuts the rope and thus cuts off the thread-life of the culprit.'

'Most commendable,' Anthom said, bowing his head as if in prayer.

Comber listened, dismayed and sickened. Both the preacher and the hangman were running the marriage and the execution of Apache Joe together, and it increased the sheriff's suspicion to notice that Kitty McGlory was totally unaffected by the talk. Everything was wrong about this, yet he had nothing on which to base an objection, to stop the little party as it made its way to the cell at the rear of the building.

'Will you join us, Sheriff Comber?' Anthom enquired with a polite smile. 'To witness this couple joined in holy matrimony?'

Shaking his head, Comber turned his back and walked to the window. Looking out, he saw the life of the town going on as normal. What was happening in his jail was unbelievable. It was only the scaffold standing on his right, complete to the last detail, ready for action, that rescued Comber from believing that he was experiencing a bad dream.

He heard voices at the back, that of the Reverend Anthom rising above all others. Then, after a long time, too long for Sheriff Comber, Anthom, Spencer, a dried-up, wizened little man, and the intense William came back into the office, having left the woman behind in the cell.

'I am sure that you will concur, Sheriff,' Anthom said in the softest voice he could manage, 'that the happy couple deserve to be alone. I have impressed upon them that what is truly a pitiful honeymoon of sorts, must last no longer than one hour.'

The clergyman, aware that he had taken a liberty, hurried off out into the street with the other two men, leaving Comber behind to fret. There was neither an exit nor an entrance at the rear of the jail, and the barred window was too small for even a midget to squeeze through.

Nevertheless, the lawman was uneasy. He berated himself for having allowed such a situation to be forced upon him, and was keenly aware of his helplessness as he paced up and down in his office.

A full hour passed by, long and fretful for the sheriff. Then, just five minutes past the deadline, he breathed an immense sigh of relief as Kitty McGlory came walking slowly out from the jail section of the building. As he relaxed at the sight of her, Comber felt a rogue wave of humour sweep over him as he recognized that she wouldn't be Kitty McGlory now. So far as the sheriff was aware, nobody knew the prisoner's name. Maybe the Reverend Anthom and Justice Spencer had improvised. If not, then this beautiful creature looking at him intently was now 'Mrs Apache Joe'.

She stood close to him, very close. Her body-warmed perfume embraced him invisibly; a sensation that turned a crusty old bachelor into a fool. Comber fought to regain his emotional balance, his mental balance, as the extraordinary woman's gaze held his as she spoke.

'You have been very kind, Sheriff,' she said, more meaning in her words because she didn't attempt a polite but insincere smile. 'Joe would like to be alone for a little while. Thank you.'

Then she was gone, out into the street and, as the door closed behind her, it was strangely as if she had never been. Sheriff Comber sat on the edge of his desk, pleading with his memory to help him conjure up the woman who had just left, but the power to do so was not there. In one crazy moment of disappointment, Comber found himself envying Apache Joe. The prisoner was a young man who was about to die on the gallows, but the sheriff wondered if a short life and a woman such as Kitty McGlory wasn't better than the long but lonely life that he had lived.

His sense of duty then put an end to what was for him an unusual romantic moment. The old unease over what had just taken place in his jail had returned to him fourfold. For all her female magic, Kitty McGlory had been all together too poised, too slick, too professional for a woman whose sole concern had been to marry an about-to-die lover. She should have been emotionally disturbed, in a terribly nervous state. But within less than an hour of her arrival in town she had the Reverend Anthom and Justice Spencer doing her bidding. In addition to that, she'd had him, the sheriff, doing exactly what she wanted him to do without him fully realizing it.

Really anxious now, he intended to ignore Apache Joe's request that he be left alone. Comber didn't want to see the young guy hanged, to be the principal player in the grim drama to come, but he would uphold the law at all costs. He was sliding down off his desk, determined to go out the back and check on his prisoner, when the door opened and Limm Sieber stepped into the office.

The bounty hunter, approaching middle age, stocky, and running a little to fat, but only to the extent that it added weight and strength to his already powerful body, wore his customary low-slung six-shooter, and also carried a rifle. He stood still inside of the door, looking at Comber, his face inscrutable by some old injury that made the tissue above his right eye droop in a way that gave him a permanent expression of bewilderment.

'What you looking for, Sieber?' a surprised sheriff asked.

After a long pause, the bounty hunter replied in a raspingly whispering voice that testified to his throat as well as his eye having at some time been injured. 'I rode in to see Apache Joe.'

'Why would you want to do that?' Comber enquired, impatient because the visitor was keeping him from checking on his prisoner.

'It's like this here, Comber,' Sieber said as he looked carefully around for somewhere to place his rifle. Satisfied to prop it against a wall, not far from him, he kept one eye on the weapon as he continued, 'Every man I ever shot and killed I was looking at. That's why I'm here.'

A lack of understanding had Comber shrug. 'You got your money for bringing the kid in, Sieber, and he'll be paying the price in about an hour's time.'

'That's the point I was making, Comber: I'm here to say a silent goodbye to Apache Joe, same's I did to the *hombres* I shot.'

Comber, still unsettled by the events of the day so far, and dreading the hanging to come, recognized some peculiar kind of chivalry in what Sieber was saying, but to him it was as chillingly eerie as the obscene enthusiasm that William had for his job as hangman.

In his own right, Limm Sieber was as much an enigma as Apache Joe. There were many stories about Sieber, but the one that seemed to fit the best was that he'd accidentally shot his young deputy during a gunfight when he'd been marshal of a town in New Mexico. Some said that the deputy had been his nephew, but Comber reckoned that was no more than an embellishment of an otherwise true tale. Since then, and nobody but Sieber himself seemed to know when it was, he had been an itinerant, a greatly feared fighting man who earned his living by bringing in those wanted by the law for serious crimes.

'I'm just going out back to take a look at Joe,' the sheriff said. 'You want to stand in the passageway to see him, Sieber?'

With a brief shake of his head, Sieber retrieved his rifle and prepared to follow the sheriff. 'That ain't my style, Comber. I'll stand up close against the bars and look him direct in the eye.'

This time it was Comber who shook his head, not in a negative way but in disbelief. 'I don't get what this is all about, Sieber.'

'How many men have you killed,

Comber?' Sieber asked, his uneven brows as disconcerting to look at as his words were to listen to.

'Nary a one, Sieber. I've been right lucky.'

Giving a curt nod of agreement on the subject of the sheriff's luck, the bounty hunter said; 'Then you won't properly understand what I'm about to say, Sheriff. The thing is, when you kills a man you've got to be there to see him off into the shadowland. It's the only way to make sure they don't come back to follow you.'

'Are any of your dead following you, Sieber?' Comber enquired, immediately regretting his question when he saw the bounty hunter instantly become dangerous. For a moment it seemed that Sieber might draw his Colt .45, or bring up the rifle he was holding, but then the moment passed.

'That's my concern, Comber,' he said, an additional hiss in his whispering voice. 'Now, you going to take me to see that kid?'

As Comber started to lead the way back to the jail, he smelled smoke at the same time as his deputy, Arthur Greening, a youngster who would still look like a schoolboy when he was fifty, came charging in through the door from the street, shouting wildly as he came.

'The back of the jailhouse is afire!' the boy was half screaming. 'It's blazing terrible, Sheriff Comber!'

A cloud of smoke and a hungrily lapping tongue of flame shot out at Comber and Sieber in immediate support of what the deputy had said. It was plain that the wooden building was ablaze and that the fire was spreading fast. Townsfolk came running with buckets of water, which were tossed on to the flames, causing no more than a hissing pause before the orange flames were leaping again.

Sheriff Comber took charge, organizing a human chain so that buckets of water were passed along continually from a source to the fire. From the shack at the bottom of town, miners came running, carrying long tin baths that slopped water as the men at each end staggered along under the weight, holding a handle that dug painfully into the hand.

'Keep 'em coming,' Comber, at the end of the line inside of the jail, Sieber in the chain next to him, called, in a coughing shout as he saw that at last, though too late, the fire was coming under control.

It was out then, with nothing more dangerous left than smouldering embers. Not much more than the framework of the building remained, and that was sagging, close to collapse. Ordering Greening to keep the crowd away, Comber, with Sieber close behind him, took a careful walk over the glowing debris towards the cells.

'Holy cow!' the sheriff gasped as he looked into the first cell, the only one that had been occupied. Lying on its back on the cot, arms composed on chest as if ready for the coffin, was the charred body of Apache Joe. What was left of the surrounding walls was blackened, and the air was so acrid that it was difficult to breathe.

'What's been going on here, Comber?' Sieber asked.

The bounty hunter walked over to the charred remains. Reaching out, he used the knuckle of a bent forefinger to lightly nudge one black arm of the corpse. Several inches of that arm, above and below the elbow, crumbled into ash, causing Sheriff Comber to give an involuntary jump. His nerves were on edge as he surveyed what had to be the outcome of his foolishness in allowing the marriage, or whatever it was, to go ahead. At least he should have been there to monitor what was going on.

'I don't know,' he replied to Sieber's question, uncertainty and worry giving his voice a tremor. 'Why would anyone want to kill a man who was to be executed within an hour?'

Swinging a surprised head in the

sheriff's direction, Sieber sharply enquired, 'Are you saying this is Apache Joe?'

First nodding, Comber then used his head to indicate the hardly burned pair of boots at the end of the cot. Flaky, charred ankles came up out of the brown boots, the leather of which had only been darkened here and there by the fire.

'Them there is Joe's boots, sure enough,' the sheriff said.

'A pair of boots don't make a man,' the bounty hunter observed grimly.

That was true, but whatever Sieber was implying couldn't alter the fact that Comber had been in the outer office at all times. The sheriff also reasoned that, if this burned body wasn't that of Apache Joe, then not only would Joe have had to have passed by him on the way out, but somehow, this body, dead or alive then, would have had to come through the front office on the way in. It just wasn't possible that those two things had occurred.

'This fella was dead before the fire,' Sieber announced as he straightened up after having studied the crisp remains. 'By the look of this mark here,' he pointed to the chest of the charred corpse, 'I'd hazard that he was knifed through the heart.'

This was bad news for Comber. It was confirmation that foul play must have somehow gone on here. But what had taken place? Lionel Anthom was a windbag who loved himself so much that God must come a poor second with him, but the sheriff couldn't accept that the preacher could be induced into any nefarious act, not even by an enchantress such as Kitty McGlory. In the same way, Justice Spencer was beyond reproach, and it wasn't likely that William would agree to anything that deprived him of a hanging. So, Comber mused, was it possible that the woman had duped the three men into helping her? This thought caused his spine to run icily cold as he recalled the effect Kitty McGlory had had on him when she had stood close on her way out. It was just possible that Apache Joe could have slipped noiselessly by them while Comber had been under her spell. But that didn't answer how whoever the dead man was had got in. Then Comber found himself shivering a little as he remembered his surprise at William being present. His suspicion aroused, he had questioned the hangman. There had been time, yes, there definitely had been time, for someone to have sneaked in through the office then. But why would a man come into the jail to be killed?

'What you intend doing about this, Sheriff?' Sieber asked as he came away from the bed.

'There'll be a hearing,' Comber shrugged, caught up in his own indecision, 'and I guess it'll be found that Apache Joe died in the fire shortly before he should have met his end on the gallows.'

'But there ain't nobody going to be able to identify what's stretched out there on the bed, fried to a doggone cinder,' Sibber protested.

With his thirty years of service running through his head in a flash, and the pleasant thought of retirement beckoning to him from a close mental horizon, Comber didn't care much right then about how things affected Limm Sieber, who was a bitter, vengeful man.

'That may be, Sieber, but it will sure do for me,' the sheriff said flatly.

'Well, Sheriff, it ain't good enough for me.' The bounty hunter turned on his heel and strode off.

Comber watched him go across the street to carve a way through a crowd of curious people. A pall of smoke hung in the air as a marker for the tragedy that had just occurred. An unhappy William was glum-faced as he studied the scaffold he had so lovingly created, but now sensed that he would never use. Arthur Greening stood with his back towards the sheriff, a rifle held across his chest as he defied an unarmed, totally harmless gathering to take a step forward.

There was no sign of Kitty McGlory among the people. If all was in order she should be in the front rank, hysterically demanding to be allowed to enter the jail where she had left her new husband. The woman's absence was enough to tell Comber that though he had seen Apache Joe's boots, it wasn't an incinerated Apache Joe who was wearing them.

Watching Limm Sieber mount a sorrel and head slowly out of town, Comber envied the man his freedom, a freedom that allowed him to ride away from the situation. No such choice was open to Comber, and his heart was heavy as he turned and walked back into his fire-wrecked office.

2

'Everyone comes *to La Rosa del Sur* seeking someone, *señor*,' the Mexican woman said to brush aside his question as she turned the register round to face him.

She was tall, middle-aged and with an elegance that placed her as the owner of the hotel. Limm Sieber realized that he couldn't offer her money for information the way he would have done a clerk. He signed his name and spun the big book back to her. Checking it, she looked directly at him for a moment. Her dark, deep eyes said more to a man in a split second than the words of an ordinary woman could say in hours. But tiredness caused Sieber to lose interest in her. It hadn't so much been the long ride that had exhausted him, but the constant buffeting of his face by wind and rain. Reaching the town in a night of unusual blackness, he had found the single street to be a quagmire.

The man at the livery where he had left his horse had been mute, either congenitally or conveniently, and now this woman had made it plain that she wouldn't respond to questions. Nevertheless, Sieber was prepared to spend one night away from the long, meandering and devious trail of Walt Traynor, an eighteen-year-old Texan who had light-blue eyes, a friendly smile, and packed a loose six-shooter.

Traynor had a high enough price on his head to make it worth Sieber's while to take him all the way back to Texas.

'It is one very bad night, *señor*,' the hotel woman commented politely as the wind rattled rain against the window behind her.

Seeing no need to reply, Sieber paid for his room and bent to pick up his bedroll. He had been aware of a Mexican *vaquero* covertly watching all the while from where he was slumped in a chair at the foot of the stairs. The gaucho looked slyly away as Sieber neared. From the *poncho* worn by the Mexican, his muddy boots and the handkerchief tied round his head, Sieber guessed he had come into town from a *parar rodeo*, the gaucho's equivalent of the cowboy's round-up.

The room was small, but only the bed interested Sieber. Most of his nights were spent outdoors, and he considered himself fortunate when he had stars and not rain or snow clouds for a ceiling. He hung his mackinaw, dripping wet, on the back of the door. There were no carpets to ruin. The bare floorboards and general austerity of the room didn't fit in with the style or the woman behind the desk downstairs. She was obviously made for better things, but that was the way of life. Sieber doubted that anyone ever found their ideal position and location in the world.

Pouring cold water from a large china jug into a basin, he stripped to the waist and began washing. There was a dark stubble on his chin, but he had arrived in town too late to find a barber. It didn't matter. One night off the trail didn't require him to be clean shaven.

The worn mirror and the dull, reflected orange glow from an oil lamp accentuated the groove a rifle bullet had carved across his throat, going on to continue the mark along his left shoulder. If he ever managed to forget that grim night, then this scar would always be there to remind him. There had been four of them, all wearing some remnant of Confederate uniform, who had ridden into town just to shoot it up. In the mêlée that followed, the usually cool-minded Sieber, anxious because of the involvement of his nephew, had been tricked into shooting him. That had been the blackest night of Limm Sieber's life. Fetching a sawn-off shotgun from his office he had killed three of the men. The fourth had got away. Sieber had only seen his back, but there was no finer way to identify a man than by his stance when seen from behind. He would know that man anywhere, and had been constantly looking for him on his travels ever since.

Resigning immediately as town marshal, Sieber had intended staying only to attend his nephew's funeral and comfort his bereaved sister, Thelma. He had remained in the town for twelve days, to bury his sister who had died of a broken heart.

As he dressed now, intending to brave the night just once more to get himself a drink, Sieber permitted himself a wry smile as Phil Comber came into his mind. The old sheriff had got what he had wanted. A jury of folk who had never set eyes on Apache Joe, returned a verdict that he had died in the jailhouse fire. Comber had been retired for more than two years now. Sieber had been considering turning it in himself, but he knew that he could never settle until the deaths of his sister and nephew had been avenged.

Going back down the stairs, stetson pulled down and the collar of his mackinaw high, ready for going out in the wet night, he found only the woman there. Behind the desk, she turned away as if fearing an inquisition from him.

Out on the street, Sieber let the lights of the town's only cantina lead him to the adobe building that was crowded and humid inside. At the bar a dark girl with Oriental features reached out a hand to place it on his arm.

'Welcome, stranger.' The girl smiled a mechanical kind of smile. 'You look like you need company.'

Shaking his arm to roughly knock the hand away, Sieber said, 'Life must sure be tough for you, gal, if it's worth your while to smile at me.'

Disappointed, a great sadness filling her eyes, the girl drew back from him so fast that it was more like a recoil.

At the bar Sieber ordered a whiskey. When the bar-keep brought him change, Sieber left it on top of the bar, tossing two dollars on to the little pile of coins and gesturing to the bartender, who was young, white and nervous, for him to pass the money along to the girl.

Accepting it eagerly, she looked along the bar at Sieber, who liked the smile that she gave him this time. He made a semi-salute to her as he raised his glass to drink, and then became aware of the man he had seen at the hotel, now coming up on his left side. The Mexican, who was not much more than a boy, had an unlit cigar clenched between his white teeth, and was proffering another cigar to Sieber.

'I will be a good friend to you, *señor.*'

Keeping his eyes straight ahead, Sieber said. 'I've already turned down the offer of a woman, *hombre.*'

'You have me wrong, *señor,*' the gaucho laughed, after first looking hurt at Sieber's assessment of him. 'I heard what you asked in the hotel, and I think that I know the man that you seek.'

Accepting the cigar, bending his head for the Mexican to light it, Sieber at the same time signalled to the barkeep. 'I'll buy you a drink, then you tell me what you know, Pedro.'

'My name is Sancho, *señor*,' the gaucho corrected him. 'Is it worth *dinero* to tell you what I know?'

'I pay for results, Sancho, not information. You take me to this man and I will pay you money.'

Gulping down his drink, Sancho explained to Sieber that he had been part of a rounding-up of cattle at El Rodeo, a vast, brown open space some miles out of town. During the *parar rodeo* a *gringo* matching the description Sieber had given the hotel woman, had ridden up and been taken on.

'He worked alongside you?' Sieber checked.

'*Si señor, si*,' Sancho nodded

vigorously. The *capataz* gave him work, but the *gringo* no good with the *lazo, señor*. I think he a *maldilo hombre*.'

All this fitted Walt Traynor. Sieber was aware that the boy from Texas hadn't been around cattle much, and he sure was a *maldito hombre* — a bad man.

'Is this man still out on the *estancias*, Sancho?'

'Si *señor*,' the Mexican replied. 'Now only he, Carlos, Luis, and me left there to tend herd. We ride out tonight, *señor*?'

'Not tonight, Sancho,' Sieber told the gaucho, who was eager to earn money. 'We'll ride out in the morning.'

'*Bueno*,' Sancho gave a beaming smile. '*Muy bueno*.'

Finishing his drink, Sieber said, 'I hope you're right. I hope that it will be very good, Sancho.'

But it wasn't. It had stopped raining during the night and they had an easy ride. Arriving at El Rodeo just before noon, they learned, to Carlos's massive disappointment, and Sieber's annoyance, that the man who fitted Walt Traynor's description had drawn his wages from the *capataz* the previous evening and had ridden off.

'He rode west,' Carlos, an elderly, grey-haired Mexican told Sieber.

The old man was squatting by a fire on which he cooked pork and beans, having already invited Sieber to join them in the meal. Luis, a tough-looking half-Indian who was probably in his mid-thirties, stood silently a little way off, neither welcoming nor rejecting Sieber. The camp included a troop of mongrel dogs, with perhaps a thin black greyhound or two among the pack. Sancho was the 'baby' of the work force, and Carlos was so fond of the young gaucho that Sieber speculated that they could be father and son.

They squatted round the fire eating. The meal was a surprisingly good one and Sieber thoroughly enjoyed it. Sancho sat next to him, seemingly in the belief that close contact might eventually lead to the payment he was hoping for. Sieber intended to give him money, for Traynor couldn't have gone far, and Carlos had revealed the direction he had taken. Maybe Sanchos wouldn't get as much as he would have if Traynor had still been in the camp, but Sieber would make sure that the young Mexican wasn't disappointed.

What interested Sieber keenly right then was the way Luis's eyes constantly scanned every horizon. The 'breed was on edge, and Sieber questioned Carlos.

'Are you expecting trouble?'

Carlos shrugged. 'Who knows? Many Indians, the Chiricahua and the Warm Springs bands, have left the agency at San Carlos and crossed the borders into the mountains of Chihuahua and Sonora. Luis expects them to raid us for these cattle.'

'Any particular reason you should think that?' Sieber asked Luis, but it was Carlos who answered.

'Luis knows these things. He come from the reservation, too. Luis rode with the San Carlos horse soldier, Apache Joe.'

Scooping up more beans, Sieber delayed speaking while he swilled them down with coffee, then he said, 'Joe being killed must have changed things for you, Luis.'

'Apache Joe dead!' Carlos was shocked, and although Luis's face remained expressionless, he swung his head to stare at Sieber.

'I thought you knew,' Sieber said. 'Happened more'n three years back.'

At this, Carlos and Luis exchanged glances, the former chuckling as he told Sieber, 'You are mistaken, *señor*. Apache Joe did not die.'

Intrigued, his suspicions about what had happened in Comber's jail confirmed, Sieber was about to ask questions but was stopped by the dogs suddenly becoming restless.

In one flowing movement Luis came upright from his hunkering position, dropping his eating irons and reaching for a rifle. Both Sanchos and Carlos stood, looking to Luis, trying to discover what was bugging him. Sieber, too, was studying the half-breed, for apart from some snarling and milling around among the pack of dogs, everything else seemed to be in order.

Then they all saw the danger that Luis had anticipated. Lining the horizon to the west, illuminated by the lowering sun behind them, was a large band of mounted Indians.

'Chiricahuas,' Luis said tersely, his voice sort of rusty from lack of use. 'Chato is leading them. They are raiding for stock.'

Going to where he had left his sorrel horse, Sieber came back carrying his rifle. Looking at him, Carlos said, 'This is not your fight, *señor.*'

'Maybe not,' Sieber muttered, then jerked his head towards the Apaches who were looking down on them. 'But those redskins aren't likely to let me ride away.'

'There's too many for us to handle,' Sancho stated the obvious.

'Do we have a choice?' Carlos asked, his lined old face creased more by worry as he looked from Sancho to the line of Indians. 'What are they waiting for?'

'They look to see how many we are,' Luis said. 'If there was enough of us to fight them, then they would stampede the herd and round it up later.'

'But now?' Sieber enquired, feeling that he already had the answer.

'Now they will run off the herd and kill us,' Luis said, as if what he was saying was of no great importance.

Hardly had the half-Indian got out the last word of his sentence when the Indians came riding in fast, whooping and hollering, startling the beef, the cows adding to the confusion with their frightened lowing and the kicking up of dust as they moved fearfully around.

As Sieber, the two Mexicans, and Luis, the half-breed, ran to their horses and hastily mounted up, so did the band of Indians divide. About twenty split away to spread out around the herd of cattle, while the remaining thirty or so came at a gallop after Sieber and the others.

The four of them rode hard, the dogs baying as they ran behind the galloping horses. The long hair of Luis streamed out behind him and the *ponchos* worn by Sancho and Carlos flopped up and down at every bound their horses made. They left the level ground of El Rodeo, riding through a waving ocean of tall grass, the horses objecting to the pace, putting up their backs, arching their necks and playing with the bit so that it jingled metallically against their teeth. But the riders fought their mounts, knowing that they had to win, to push the animals on as fast as possible. Luis rode well, his horse a dark dun, with eyes of fire, a black stripe down its back, and a long tail that floated out straight in the wind and helped its rider in his turnings.

Down a steep slope they went, the

dogs keeping up, tongues lolling out of their mouths droolingly. All the time there came the thunder of the hooves of the Apaches' ponies behind them, seemingly growing louder by the second. They crashed through thick cane-brakes, across the deltas of streams, splashing through the streams themselves, and then they came up out of an arroyo and saw up ahead a prairie camp.

It was three small buildings made of adobe bricks of sunbaked earth, but it was a sight that offered them refuge. Dismounting fast, they tied their horses at the rear of the buildings, then crowded into one, the dogs following them, men and beasts seeking sanctuary within the adobe walls.

The Apaches, apparently undecided as to their next move, stayed a little way off, out of effective range. All four of them were sweating hard after the frantic ride, and the air was hot and oppressive. Luis looked out of the window at the pump that was a hundred feet away, and then looked down at the empty water bucket resting against a wall.

'If we're going to be holed up here, then we'll need water,' the half-breed said.

Carlos picked up the bucket. 'It is best to go now before the Chiricahua move in on us. I will go, for I have the least number of years left, being the oldest.'

'You're the oldest and the slowest, Carlos,' Luis rebuked him, as he took the bucket away from the older man.

The half-breed walked calmly out of the door, swinging the bucket, as unconcerned as a home-steader going out on his place to milk the family cow. Completing the peaceful scene was the dog that followed Luis, head drooping as it walked at heel.

Just as Luis hung the bucket on the pump spout, a volley of shots rang out and the dog flopped into the dust, riddled with bullets. A slug whipped off Luis's hat, and bullets whistled around him as he worked the handle of the pump up and down. With bullets spitting all around him, the half-breed kept pumping until the bucket was full of water. Then stooping to pick up his hat, he walked casually back to the building.

When he came in, he placed the bucket on the floor and observed with regret, 'I sure wish that dawg hadn't followed me.'

Sieber, who was at the window with his rifle hoping for a glimpse of a redskin target, glanced quickly and admiringly at Luis. Of all the scrapes he had been in, and all the fighting men he had been with and against, he had never witnessed anything so cool as what the half-breed had just done.

Carlos gave Sieber a lopsided grin and told him, 'We must give thanks to *Madre de Dios, señor*, that Luis is in here fighting with us, and not out there against us.'

That was a sentiment Sieber fully agreed with, and he shared grins with

46

Carlos and Sancho. Luis just smiled at him with his eyes, very briefly.

Dusk was thickening, making it difficult to see any reasonable distance, when a sudden realization had Sieber curse himself. He had left ammunition for his rifle in his saddle pack out back.

'Don't worry,' Carlos said, when Sieber spoke of his mistake. 'Night is coming now, so you won't need a rifle. When these Chiricahuas come at us we will be doing our fighting hand-to-hand.'

'I'll . . . ' Luis started to say, moving off towards the door, but Sieber grabbed his arms and pulled him back.

Slipping out into the night, he found it to be so quiet that it didn't seem possible that it held any danger. But, as a veteran, Sieber knew differently. As he rounded the corner of the building an Apache rose up out of a clump of weeds and fired at him. The bullet passed by, scraping the side of Sieber's head as it went, but not close enough either to break the skin or stun him. The Indian was levelling his rifle for a second shot when Sieber leapt forward to grab the weapon by the barrel. tugging hard and fast, yanking the Apache towards him, Sieber raised his elbow, feeling it find the Indian's nose, hitting the bone so hard that it drove it up into the forehead.

With the Indian gurgling and choking on his own blood, Sieber got round behind him, held the rifle across his throat then pulled on it to crush the Apache's windpipe.

Letting the dead man drop, Sieber felt bullets come from somewhere to cut his clothing. Then an Indian landed on his back, smashing him face first against the adobe wall. He went flat down onto the ground, head spinning but able to feel powerful bare arms circle his throat, pulling his head back, cutting off his breathing so that his head really began to swim. When he tried to fight back he found he had no strength. He was aware of one arm releasing him, then he knew why as he felt a knife hitting him hard on the left side, coming through his clothing and slicing the skin as it was aimed to go between his ribs and into his heart.

Sieber knew that it was all over for him, then he heard a hollow cracking sound while at the same time he was freed. Rolling on to his back, Sieber looked up to see Luis above him, and he realized that the half-breed had clubbed the Indian, and the sound Sieber had heard was the Apache's skull splitting.

'Inside,' Luis said, reaching down a hand to pull Sieber groggily to his feet. 'We won't be fighting with rifles.'

Back inside the four six-shooters of Sieber, Luis, and the two Mexicans, all the guns being .45 calibre, were pooled. Sieber and Luis took up firing positions by the window, while Carlos and Sancho stayed just behind to reload and pass the guns back.

They were organized just in time, for

the first wave of Apaches hit them hard and fast. They came on foot, charging at the window. At times there were four Indians at once with their rifle barrels at the windows, with others behind ready to move in when those in front were brought down by fire from Sieber and Luis. It was only the speed of their six-shooters and the rapid reloading behind them that kept the Apaches at bay. They had closed and barred the door, which narrowed down the scope for the Indians' attack.

The Apaches dropped back to regroup then, leaving a pile of dead and wheezing, groaning, bleeding, and sometimes screaming, wounded behind them. With a plentiful supply of ammunition for their .45s, the four men in the adobe building were confident that they could hold out indefinitely. The night was cool, but when the heat of the day did arrive, they had water, thanks to Luis. All of them were accustomed to going without food for long periods, so that prospect didn't worry them.

When the Apaches charged again they were on their ponies. They circled the building, unmindful of their number that were being cut down by the accurate fire of Sieber and Luis. The Indians poured lead and arrows against the earthen walls, the impact of the missiles knocking lumps out of the sun-baked bricks.

One Indian, a young man whose eyes were staring wide, and teeth bared in a snarl, sent his panicking pony straight at the window.

Sieber shot the pony between the eyes, and it was dropping as it crashed into the front of the building. The impact caused the whole wall to shudder, and the Apache was catapulted straight in through the window, flying over the heads of Sieber and Luis, going between Carlos and Sancho, to slam against the rear wall and fall back on to the floor.

Quick as a flash, the Apache did a sideways roll and was coming up off the floor. He had lost his rifle in the fall, but was holding a wicked-bladed knife.

Turning, Sieber aimed his .45 at the dangerous Apache, but the two Mexicans were so close that a shot couldn't be risked. He was reversing his gun, hoping to be able to hold the barrel and use it as a club, when Luis stepped quickly past him to shoot out a foot that connected with the Indian's wrist, knocking the knife out of his hand. Another looping kick from Luis caught the Apache behind the knees, dropping him. Even as the Indian hit the floor, Luis was on his back, pulling his head back, snapping the Apache's neck, picking the dead Indian up by his hair and breech-clouts to throw him effortlessly head first back out of the window.

It went quiet then, with the Chiricahuas staying away, licking their wounds as they planned the next attack. With time to think, Sieber rued the circumstances that trapped him there when he should have been hot on Walt Traynor's trail. He turned his mind to Luis then. Never had he seen a man able to handle himself so speedily and effectively. It was fortunate, Sieber told himself, that in his long years as a bounty hunter he hadn't encountered a fighting man such as Luis was.

Taking a loaded gun from Sancho, Sieber remarked to Luis, 'You handle yourself real well.'

'I had a good teacher,' Luis replied, without taking his eyes away from where the Apaches would come charging out of the darkness again.

'Apache Joe?' Sieber asked, and the fact that Luis didn't answer was enough to tell him he had guessed rightly. The puzzle was why Apache Joe had given up so easily when Sieber had caught up with him. Come to that, the renegade was a mystery all round, for what had taken place in Phil Comber's jail defied explanation.

There was no further conversation

from then on as the dark hours passed. It was just after dawn that the Chiricahuas next attacked, riding in out of the sun in force.

Again they rained bullets and arrows against the walls. They circled in close, not worried by the deadly fire from Sieber and Luis. Some dismounted to one side and ran at the window, but not one was able to get so much as a hand inside of the building before dying.

An Indian backed his horse skilfully and heavily against the barred door, all but breaking it in before Sieber shot him in the head. Another was on the earthen roof, frantically digging a hole in it. They could hear but not place him until a shower of sunbaked earth fell, followed by an arrow that, although aimed indiscriminately, entered downwards into the top of Sancho's chest, going downwards through his body. Sancho fell, blood running thickly from one side of his mouth as Carlos caught him in his arms, going down on his knees to support the badly wounded young gaucho.

While this was going on, both Sieber and Luis fired up through the hole in the roof, being rewarded by a grunt of pain and then the slithering sound of a body slipping down the roof and falling off.

Determined to end the siege, the Apaches were sacrificing man after man, when a volley of shots from further away slowed them down and they started to look behind them.

Still kneeling with the stricken Sancho in his arms, Carlos guessed what was happening outside. 'The *capataz* has come back with the rest of the *vaqueros* to fetch the herd.'

This was true. The Mexican foreman of the round-up came riding in at the head of his men, all guns blazing, causing the Chiricahuas to gallop away.

Soon the adobe building was crowded with *vaqueros*, and Sieber had to push his way to stand above Carlos and Sancho. Taking a bill-roll from his pocket, Sieber peeled of some banknotes and leaned forward to hold them out to Carlos.

'I owe the boy,' Sieber said.

Looking up through moist eyes, the old Mexican spoke in a voice choked by emotion, 'Sancho will not need *dinero* where he is going, *señor*.'

The face of the young Mexican was ashen, contrasting starkly with the blood of a darker red that was now leaking more heavily from his mouth. Sieber had to agree with the old Mexican, money would never again be of any use to Sancho.

'Is he your . . . ?' Sieber was saying when Carlos pre-empted him.

'*Si, señor*.'

'I'm real sorry, Carlos.'

'*Si, señor*,' a grieving Carlos said again, and Sieber found that he had to walk away from the sorrowful scene.

At the back of the building he discovered that, miraculously, his roan had survived without a scratch. Luis was there, mounting his dun in the way peculiar to Mexicans, in one motion bending a knee to pass it over the middle of the saddle, but never dwelling in the stirrup after the European way.

Extending his right hand up to the half-breed, Sieber wore a wry grin as he enquired, 'Should I say *hasta la vista*, Luis?'

Shrugging to show his indecision as to whether or not it would be a good thing for Sieber and himself to meet again, Luis took the proffered hand but kept his eyes on a distant horizon.

'You fight well, Sieber, which makes you worth knowing,' the half-breed said, as he released Sieber's hand and sat upright in the saddle.

An afterthought made Sieber turn back. 'What if I was to ask you the last time you saw Apache Joe, Luis?'

Moving his horse slowly away, the half-breed said without looking back, 'You did not get to know me very well if you expect me to answer, Sieber.'

'It was worth a try,' Sieber said, adding, although the half-breed didn't hear because he had ridden out of earshot, 'I got to know you pretty well, Luis.'

3

As celebrities they were invited to dine in the officers' mess at Fort Laramie. It was surprisingly well furnished and decorated for a frontier army post; a spearhead of civilization and sophistication aided by a trio of male musicians. The tune they played was the ghost of a safer, saner time past, come to haunt folk who, though military, were uneasy dwelling in so harsh a land. There were four other women there, army wives, but the flame-haired Kitty McGlory was the centre of attention. The younger, unattached officers at the table struggled to conceal their interest in her, at all times keenly aware of her dark, brooding husband sitting at her side. Even the formal dinner had not deterred Joe McGlory from wearing his .38 six-shooter low on his thigh, tied there by a leather thong. For all the boyishness imparted by his lithe physique and the way his short, black hair was neatly cut, McGlory had a menacing aura. To those who knew the West and the characters who peopled it, which included every officer at the table, it was plain that Joe McGlory had killed many times in the past and would have no compunction in killing again if he deemed it necessary.

Kitty felt good sitting there on equal terms with Colonel Nelson Wright, who commanded the fort. She was under no illusion that the colonel, a man whose prominent-nosed face gained an added severity from a heavy, grey moustache, would not have given either Joe or herself the time of day before they had ridden into Fort Worth with $10,000 in their saddle-bags. At Worth they had sunk most of that money into a herd of one thousand longhorns, then had taken on twenty cowboys, a cook, a horse wrangler, three bullwhackers, and a fast-spreading fame when it was learned they intended to drive the herd to Montana.

So far they had enjoyed a leisurely move along the old Oregon Trail across Kansas and Nebraska, arriving at Fort Laramie for a short break while restocking the groceries carried on three ox-drawn wagons. While at the fort they had been warned constantly that their bad times were about to begin, and the commanding officer took up the same theme now.

'I would advise you to listen to Captain Flynn, who is a most experienced officer, Mr McGlory,' Colonel Wright said solemnly, and Kitty, as always, had to suppress a grin at hearing her husband called by her surname. 'The Sioux and Cheyenne are swarming all over central Wyoming.'

'That's true,' agreed Flynn, a young officer who sat with his wife. She must have been at least ten years his senior, although she retained an attractiveness.

While speaking, Flynn had covertly

glanced in Kitty's direction. As flattered by this sort of thing as any woman would be, she reminded herself that it probably sprang less from her physical attraction than it did from the fact that she was the first woman ever to go on a cattle drive. Occasionally she had ridden a horse along the trail, but mostly she used a buggy.

'I don't think we'll have much trouble, Colonel,' Joe McGlory said, better able to carry on a conversation these days, but still too taciturn for his wife's liking. 'I picked my men carefully, as I imagine you do for a special detail, and we have armed all of them with new Remington, rapid-fire, breech-loading rifles.'

'Be that as it may,' Captain Flynn conceded in part, 'it remains a fact that the Indians fiercely attack anything that moves out there on Bozeman Trail.'

Joe McGlory delayed answering while Colonel Wright signalled to a waiter for more wine, indicating that he should first replenish Kitty's glass and then those of the other ladies. Then, his face taking on an even greater Indian appearance in the subdued lighting, Joe said quietly, 'Nothing we meet on the Bozeman Trail will prevent me from selling our beef at a handsome profit in the north-western mining camps of Montana, Captain.'

'I pray that nothing will, Mr McGlory,' the colonel put in. 'I confess that the action we have taken, the building of three forts along the trail, has only served to exacerbate the situation. We upset the tribes so that they have merged into one fighting forge under the leadership of Chief Red Cloud.'

'With respect, sir,' a thin, ailing-looking major of around the commanding officer's age ventured, 'should we engage in such alarmist talk in the presence of ladies in general, and Mrs McGlory in particular?'

As he answered this modest challenge, Colonel Wright looked steadily at Kitty. 'I do take your point, Major Gregory, and I empathize to some extent.

However, I firmly believe it to be my bounden duty to persuade, deter, or whatever, our guests from making so perilous a drive to Montana.'

'I have faith in the project,' Major Gregory persisted. 'I understand that there are more than a hundred thousand cattle held up by the Jayhawkers' barricade in Kansas, so Mr McGlory's decision to divert is commendable.'

'I can't take credit for the detour, Major, that was my wife's notion.' Joe McGlory gave a rare and sparse smile. They had been aware of the farmers who had settled land from Baxter Springs north-eastward to the Sedalia railhead, blocking herds from using their land. It was said that they didn't want their crops trampled and fences knocked down, and that they also had a fear of the fatal cattle disease of Spanish or Texas fever being spread by ticks carried on Texan cows. The truth was probably that the Kansas farmers, who had been on the Union side in the war, just didn't like Texans.

Regardless of the reason or reasons for the barricade, Kitty was adamant that they wouldn't waste time with it, so she had said they would go round.

'So, Clive,' Colonel Wright gave Major Gregory a weak smile, as if he would dearly love to share in Gregory's optimism, 'you are of the opinion that Mr and Mrs McGlory will reach Montana and sell their cattle?'

'If it can be done, then I believe that they are the people to do it,' the major replied.

'I'm inclined to agree with you, Clive,' the commanding officer said before looking at Joe and Kitty with admiration in his eyes, and perhaps a degree of fondness. 'If I cannot stay you, my good people, then I must join Major Gregory in wishing you good fortune all along the way.'

There were gasps of horror from the women, including his own wife, when Captain Flynn exclaimed, 'There is no good fortune, nor good anything else along the Bozeman Trail. Good God,

65

gentlemen, you know as well as I do that Red Cloud will stampede their cattle and take their scalps for good measure.'

'This is extremely bad form, Captain,' Gregory protested, jumping to his feet, chin quivering with indignation and anger.

'I cannot issue a formal reprimand in the mess, Captain Flynn, but I think it prudent to ask that you apologize to our guests for what must, at the very least, be sheer bad taste,' Colonel Wright, his face a little white, said before turning to Kitty and Joe. 'It is my regret if you have been offended by my officer's words.'

Inclining his dark head a little to one side, Joe McGlory said, 'No offence taken, Colonel. I never object to anything a man says as long as it's the truth. Captain Flynn doesn't think we have a chance, and he said so. I can't see anything wrong in that.'

'Your forbearance is very much appreciated, Mr McGlory,' the colonel told Joe while he bestowed a warm smile upon Kitty. 'I feel it necessary to stay in my role as a Jonah just a while longer to caution that you can expect little or no protection or support from the army along the Bozeman Trail. This is due to the fact that we are stretched far and beyond the limit.'

'We understand that, Colonel, and would stress that we would not wish to jeopardize the lives of soldiers to achieve our business aims,' Kitty said.

'A most noble and principled attitude,' Major Gregory said with a smile that stretched the skin so tightly over his bony face that it seemed in danger of splitting.

'I agree, but out here I feel that we are all responsible for one another, regardless of individual ambitions,' Colonel Wright nodded. 'That is why I will see you off in the morning with a heavy heart.'

'As my wife has said, we are taking this on ourselves and would not wish to have anyone taking any risks, or worrying unduly on our behalf. Our men were told what to expect before they signed on for the drive, and they are being paid over the top,' Joe McGlory said in what for him was a long speech.

Getting to his feet, a hand under his wife's elbow to assist her from her seat, Captain Flynn prepared to leave, bowing first to the ladies and then Colonel Wright. 'If you will excuse us, ladies, sir.' He stepped towards Kitty and Joe McGlory, who rose up to shake his hand as Flynn went on, 'Forgive me for not being there when you move out on the morrow. Having given my warning I feel it would be hypocritical of me to salute your departure when convinced that only grief awaits you. Of course, this in no way means that you won't constantly be in our prayers. God speed.'

'I will ask the Lord to keep you safe,' Captain Flynn's wife said shyly as she shook them by the hand, dropping a little half-curtsy for Kitty as if she was of royal blood.

'Might I suggest,' Colonel Wright said, when the Flynns had left the mess, 'that we have one last drink together.' He turned to the three-man orchestra. 'End the evening for us in a special way, gentlemen, by playing my favourite, 'Beautiful Dreamer'.' He became embarrassed, almost gauche, when he smiled at Kitty and said, 'A most fitting title, I feel.'

'A compliment indeed, sir,' Kitty smiled back prettily. 'I will make you a promise, Colonel Wright: hold a ball when we come back down the Bozeman Trail, and I will dance with you to that tune.'

The colonel bowed deeply. 'I shall anticipate that occasion with the utmost pleasure, madam, providing that Mr McGlory will have no objection?'

'When we come back down the trail,' McGlory said, 'I guess I'll be ready to dance with you myself, Colonel.'

'I'd prefer it to be Mrs McGlory,'

the colonel said, tongue-in-cheek and a twinkle in his eye.

That ended the evening with a laugh, but it was a serious business when the herd moved off the next morning. Soldiers and civilians watched with interest. The McGlory cowboys had made an early start, the smell of cooking had come from the chuck-wagon before dawn, and before it was light the cook's cry of 'Arise and shine! Come and get it!' had echoed around outside of the fort. All hands on the drive travelled light, the McGlorys permitting them each a pair of bed blankets and a sack in which they carried a small amount of spare clothing. They took no means of shelter for along the trail, no tents. All that would be between them and the elements were the two blankets.

In his silent, methodical way, Joe McGlory had organized everything well. The watching military men recognized that they were observing an operation every bit as complex as starting an army off on a march. McGlory had wisely selected a huge aggressive animal, a beast that commanded respect from the other cattle, and made it the lead steer. There were no hurried movements, no rush, for the herd had to once more become accustomed to the disciplined routine of the drive. Where grass was available cows were allowed to graze before gently being moved on.

Having said their goodbyes and conveyed their thanks for the hospitality at the fort, Joe and Kitty McGlory were riding in advance of the herd, he on a black stallion, she in her buggy.

Directly behind them came the cook driving his kitchen on wheels, while to his left was the horse wrangler with the remuda. There were more than a hundred horses here, for the long ride ahead with a diet comprising only wild prairie grass, meant that the cowhands would need to change mounts frequently if the horses were to be kept in good condition. Then came the point, with the lead steer and the finest specimens in the herd, and the point riders on each side. Then came the thick body of cattle, kept from spreading too wide by the flank riders, winding the drive this way and that like a huge lazy snake, with the drag riders, bandannas over their mouths and noses to keep out the dust, bringing up the tail.

It was quite a sight that bright and cheerful morning, although the sun was making a promise that it wouldn't be able to keep for many more hours. Dark rainclouds lay threateningly on the eastern horizon, gaining more sky surreptitiously so that the riders were surprised, and disheartened, each time they took a look skywards.

Within an hour, a drizzling rain was whispering of worse to come. The McGlorys pushed on. Now that the cattle were finding their pace and place in the herd, progress was faster and, if the rain permitted, they felt sure that they would cover the ten miles they had planned for that day. They kept going although the rain poured down in torrents. It was a relief for everyone when the rain eased off just before Joe McGlory called a halt.

As Clancy Magee got a fire of buffalo chips going and then the smell of cooking permeated the air, Joe McGlory supervised the bedding down of the herd for the night. He divided the night watch into shifts of two hours duration, which brought a mild protest from a young cowpuncher who was disfigured by a broken nose.

'Us boys would prefer to do four hours, Joe. That way some of us can get a full night's sleep.'

'Two hours,' Joe said firmly as he walked away, raising an arm to where lightning crackled, joining distant earth and land with darting, bright yellow streaks. 'That way you'll stay alert. We don't want a stampede tonight or any other night.'

Going to the chuckwagon he got two plates of food and carried them across to where Kitty sat with her back against one wheel of the buggy. Squatting beside her, he passed over one of the plates. They ate in silence, both just conveying their thanks with a nod when Magee brought them a mug of coffee each.

When they had finished eating, Kitty held her steaming mug with both hands, breathing in the coffee before drinking it, looking straight ahead as she spoke.

'Everyone back at Fort Laramie is sure we aren't going to make it, Joe.'

Snatches of melancholy ballads were reaching them now as the night herders serenaded the cattle to pacify them. It was all very commonplace to Joe, who had known cattle drives before, but it was totally alien to Kitty. When they had met she had been owner of the Five Points saloon in Santa Fe. It was a low establishment that thrived on the patronage of thugs — the gunmen and gangsters who were unwelcome in most other places. The dance-hall girls in the Five Points were the low type that made it a den of vice. Only the brave ventured in through the doorway and along the dark passage that led to the saloon and the hall beyond. The chairs and tables were greasy and damaged. Where repairs had been carried out they had been done with clumsy ineptitude. The balcony running along the sides of the hall had been partitioned into small compartments by heavy, fetid, musty curtains. A three-piece orchestra that nobody listened to was made up of a piano, cornet, and violin. Order was maintained by a gang of gunmen and manhandlers employed by Kitty McGlory.

There was nothing squeamish about Five Points; no pretence at modesty in either the singing or the dancing. The girls brazenly asked for coins to be put in their stockings, and there was no shortage of males eager to oblige, usually with a quarter that they fumbled against fleshy thighs to press into place. It cost a lot more to go to one of the curtained compartments with one of the girls, although the transaction there was concluded almost as quickly as the coin in a stocking escapade.

It was a place that had earned Kitty McGlory an undeserved reputation, and had made her a rich woman. It was a place where the renegade Apache Joe had known he could enjoy anonymity. He had made just one visit, but that had been enough for Kitty to fall heavily for him. As drawn to her as she was to him, he had been candid about his circumstances. He had explained that even had he wished to stay in one place, which he most certainly didn't, it would be impossible because the law would find him. Declaring that she would follow him to the ends of the earth if necessary, Kitty had sold up and had found herself following him no further than to a sheriff's office where a bounty hunter had imprisoned him.

When Kitty had rescued him they had sought a way of life which wouldn't separate them. Pooling the money she had obtained from vice and he from outlawry, they had gone into the cattle business in a way that catered for the need for adventure that was in both of them.

'Let them think what they like,' he said, making a cigarette and lighting it.

'And what do you think?' she asked, brows knitting a little, an indication that his answer was important to her.

'I think,' he said evenly, 'that I'll get this herd to Montana or die in the attempt. Does that worry you, Kitty?'

They both tensed as thunder rattled, unannounced by lightning, and the herd stirred in fear. The night herders sang and made placating noises, and they were relieved by sounds that told them that the cattle were settling down.

'It doesn't worry me at all, Joe,' she told him quietly. 'For if you die, then I will die by your side. We will be together into eternity.'

Rain began to fall again, and they heard the cook curse roundly about it because he hadn't finished his chores. Reaching for their blankets, Joe McClory said; 'Come on, we'll be drier if we sleep under one of the ox-wagons.'

'No.' She put a restraining hand on his arm. 'We'd be too close to the others, Joe. Let's stay here, together.'

4

The long pursuit of Walt Traynor had been drawing to a close when everything had gone wrong for Limm Sieber. Although cautious and cunning, at all times careful to cover his tracks, Traynor had given way to a minor panic on realizing that Sieber was trailing him. Moving his horse fast across the plain, Traynor had run into a *cangrejal*, a colony of land crabs, a very dangerous trap for riders. Breaking a foreleg as it went down, Traynor's horse had thrown him. Coming up awkwardly on to three legs, the broken one swinging loosely and uselessly, the horse had fallen around shrieking before Traynor had put it out of its suffering by shooting it. Holding back, Sieber had kept out of sight, lying in some dunes where he was able to watch Traynor, who all the time kept a wary eye behind him, take the saddle off the dead horse, swing it up on to his shoulder and walk off awkwardly in his high-heeled boots.

Intending to follow, Sieber was in no hurry. Texas was a long way back, and he'd never reach there with Traynor on foot. He was relying on the ruthless and resourceful Texan to get himself another horse. That was when Sieber would move in and take the wanted man. He would do it craftily, avoiding gunplay, for there was no way he was going to tote a dead man through the heat all the way to Texas.

He lay back for a while, tilting his stetson over his face to shield it from the sun. Relaxing, Sieber dozed a little. When he raised himself up it was to see Traynor, no more than a tiny dot, dropping over a very distant horizon.

Mounting up, Sieber rode slowly on. At a walking pace he went through a divide, his ears catching the clip of a horseshoe on rock before he reached the end. Pushing his horse steadily up over a hog-back, he reined up and looked with surprise at the scene below him.

A battered old wagon with a pair of semi emaciated ponies had pulled up and Traynor, hands on his hips, saddle on the ground by his feet, was looking up at the elderly man and youngish woman sitting up on the seat. Unable to make out the words, Sieber judged that some kind of bargaining was taking place between Traynor and the old man. Chuckling in some kind of pretend or half-amusement, the oldster climbed down, shaking his head as Traynor held out money to him.

When Traynor took his hand out of his pocket the next time, now obviously holding more money, Sieber saw the old man give a quick nod of agreement. Assuming that Traynor had purchased one of the ponies, and wondering how the remaining half-starved beast would manage to pull the wagon alone, Sieber was astonished when the elderly man beckoned impatiently to the woman, and she climbed down reluctantly from the wagon.

The woman stood docilely, head down on her large, firm bosom, as Sieber saw the old man point to a cluster of trees some ten yards away. Nodding, Traynor slipped an arm around the woman's waist. Sieber could see her cringe and her body go rigid, but Traynor used the arm around her waist to move her towards the trees.

As the couple went off, the old man, chuckling with pleasure loud enough for Sieber to hear, pulled a little bulging sack from his pocket and started to push the money Traynor had given him into the poke.

Releasing the woman Traynor took three or four quick steps back to the elderly man. Putting his six-shooter against the back of the greying old head, Traynor pulled the trigger to blow the old man's brains out messily.

As the old fellow fell dead to the ground, the woman didn't scream as

Sieber had expected her to. She just stood swaying, a hand clapped over her mouth.

Going to her, still holding his gun in his hand, Traynor gestured for her to get back up on to the seat of the wagon. She obeyed as Traynor bent to pick up his saddle and toss it into the bed of the wagon. Then he, too, climbed up onto the seat. Starting to reach for the reins, Traynor changed his mind, and Sieber saw him grab the woman sitting beside him. He heard the sound of tearing material, and the woman did scream then, but Traynor just gave a wild laugh.

Digging in his spurs, Sieber sent his horse over the hog-back galloping down at the stationary wagon. First releasing the woman, who immediately tried to put her torn dress together, Traynor then quickly scrambled behind her, putting an arm round her throat, using her as an effective shield.

Reining up, Sieber dismounted. Traynor was holding a gun on him, but he made no attempt to draw as he walked up. All that was showing was half of Traynor's good-looking face, with one eye showing, bright-blue, just like it said on the reward dodger. The Texan's hat had been knocked back to put corn-coloured hair on show. Cut short, it was formed into tight curls of the same size all over his head.

'Stop right there, mister,' Traynor drawled. 'Iffen you don't, then I'll plug yer between the eyes, and you sure ain't going to be able to rescue the little woman then.'

Standing still, Sieber knew that he had to take a chance. The kid had the drop on him, and it was only a matter of a short time before Traynor got out of the situation by killing him. Delay was futile, but action was risky. There was no guarantee that the woman wouldn't move a little, or Traynor move her. The arm was choking her, but Sieber was struck by her attractive face. She was younger than he had estimated from a distance.

'You've been following me for quite a spell, ain't you, *hombre*?' Traynor said accusingly.

'That's true,' Sieber conceded. 'I guess I kind of got to know you, in a way. That's what had me figure we can come to some sort of arrangement here.'

Giving a short, harsh laugh, the Texan said, 'Don't seem to me that ye're in a position to talk about arrangements being made, mister.'

'Well, the way I see it . . . ' Sieber began, getting Traynor's attention, then drawing his .45, firing, and taking a step to one side all in one motion.

A yell of sheer terror came from the woman, freezing Sieber's heart, but then he saw the single bright-blue eye go out like a light. There was no more than a messy hollow there, squirting out blood so that the woman's face looked as if she had been hit.

But Traynor fell backwards, dropping dead into the wagon, while Sieber just had time to reholster his gun and step forwards to catch the woman in both arms as she toppled from the wagon in a dead faint. Lowering the unconscious woman to the ground, Sieber checked on Traynor, whose bottom half lay on the seat, right leg twisted awkwardly underneath, while the top of his body dangled, his head hanging loosely, mouth agape, remaining blue eye wide as it stared fixedly at his last moment alive on earth. He was as dead as the old fellow whose brains he had blown out.

Unhooking Traynor's right leg, which was all that kept him up on the seat, Sieber let the body crash to the ground, then climbed up and looked into the wagon. It contained all the ugly, worn, and unclean trappings of an impoverished lifestyle. Sickened by the squalor, Sieber stepped back down to the ground as the woman began to stir feebly.

Getting his canteen of water, he slipped off his bandanna as he knelt beside her. Soaking the material in water, he first washed the clots of Traynor's blood from the side of her face, then tenderly bathed her forehead and closed eyes. Her body was well-fleshed, and her roughened hands told Sieber that she was more accustomed to doing hard chores than earning in the way she had been forced into with Traynor. She must have been a good thirty years younger than the old man, but she had symmetrical features, a loveliness now that unconsciousness had taken the strain from her face, whereas the old man was ugly. Accepting that this didn't mean that she wasn't his daughter, Sieber thought it unlikely.

Her eyes blinked open normally, then widened in fright as she saw him bending over her, his face close. Pulling back, Sieber spoke soothingly. 'It's all right, ma'am, take it real easy now, you're safe.'

With Sieber's help the woman sat up. Looking round, first at the dead Traynor, then at the body of the old man, she studied Sieber critically, plainly trying to work out where he fitted into the grim little scenario. He was wondering, too, bitterly. Having spent a great deal of time tracking down Traynor, and coming close to losing his life when with the Mexicans, it was hard to accept that it was all for naught. A dead Walt Traynor this far from Texas wasn't worth a dime.

'Have you got a name?' he asked, as he helped her to her feet, keeping a supporting hand on her arm because she was unsteady.

Nodding, she replied, 'Judy.'

'Well, Judy, what are we going to do?' he asked the question of himself, not her, speaking softly. Gesturing to the old man, he asked, 'Was he kin?'

'No.' She shook her head, shuddering, her head and shoulders first, then her whole body was shaking uncontrollably. When it was over she continued, 'I was with him because I had no choice. My family were . . . '

She broke off there, but Sieber had

got the picture. Something terrible had happened to her family. Something so bad that she couldn't put it into words, and he doubted that she would ever be able to. Maybe it was Indians, perhaps outlaws. Whatever, she had been left alone in a vast wilderness. She must have come upon the old man by chance. Travelling with him, although it must have been a hideous experience, was probably preferable to a woman than being alone.

'You heading anywhere in particular, Judy?' he enquired delicately, anxious not to upset her with any unintentional reminders of her plight.

'No, sir, I . . . '

'My name's Limm,' he told her. 'Call me Limm.'

She nodded, too enthusiastically, as if calling him by name was the most exciting thing that had happened to her in a long while. It was evidence of the state she was in. Her massive shuddering had stopped, but he could see the tiny tremors running through her body. It wasn't cold, so fear had to be the cause. In her vulnerable position she was as terrified of him as she had been the elderly man she'd been travelling with.

'I ain't got no place nowhere to go, Limm,' she said, speaking his name in such a low voice that he wasn't sure he had heard it.

Looking up at the sun, which was only just past the late-day side of its zenith, he told her, 'Well, Judy, I guess we're both wanderers right now, but we've got to go some place.'

Climbing up into the wagon he began the distasteful job of clearing it, using his feet to kick all of the old man's stuff out the back on to the ground. Then he walked to her, and she cringed away from him.

'I won't harm you, Judy, not in any way,' he assured her. 'Now, let me help you up on to the seat and we'll make tracks out of here.'

When she was seated, Sieber led his horse to the rear of the wagon and tied it to the tailgate. Stepping over the body of Traynor, he bent to remove the well-filled little sack of money from the pocket of the elderly man, then gestured at the body with a tilt of his head.

'Would you want me to bury him, Judy?'

'No,' she replied, quickly and emphatically.

'You're right, and the other *hombre* don't deserve it either,' he said as he swung himself up and took the reins.

Helped by the rest, the two scraggy ponies moved the wagon off. This was strange country to Sieber, but his experience of life in the great outdoors strongly suggested that if he was to head south-west he would pick up the Bozeman Trail. From then on they would just have to keep moving until they came to one of the army's forts. Once there he could leave Judy in safety before deciding his own immediate future. It seemed likely that he would need to take on a job with a rancher so as to build up his finances before going back to his regular occupation.

If Traynor was the worst thing ever to have happened to him, then he had a feeling, ridiculous though it was, that the woman beside him might well turn out to be more than adequate compensation. From the corner of his eye he could see her in profile. Sorrow was etched on her face, but there was a strength there. They hadn't spoken since he had set the wagon moving, but somehow that was difficult to believe. It was as if there was some kind of silent communication between them that made them content to remain silent. In a way, Sieber reasoned, words would spoil everything.

Yet he had to speak to tell her his plans as they zigzagged up a creek. 'If we can get the wagon through that timber up ahead, Judy, then we'll take a rest the other side. I've water and some dried meat in my saddlebags behind.'

'If we can't get through the timber?' she enquired.

'Then it will take us a fair while, but we'll go round it and then pull in,' he replied.

They were in luck. The going was rough over a deer trail through young timber, but it was wide enough for the wagon. Yet Limm Sieber, strictly an open-space man, was on edge as they moved with the wagon jolting and rattling along the rough track through the woods. The feeling of oppressive confinement among the trees was developing into a sense of menace in Sieber, and he was glad that he had brought his rifle up on to the wagon seat with him. It lay between Judy and himself, a welcome assurance in the sight of it.

The sun coming through the trees created shifting patterns of light and shadow that the tense Sieber found to be disconcerting. Judy sat silent at his side, head high, eyes flicking this way and that in alertness. He surmised that she might be sharing the unease that he felt, or perhaps her nerves were still reacting to her recent experiences.

A moving shadow beside a tree up ahead became an armed Indian too quickly for Sieber either to reach for his rifle or draw his .45. The redskin had a rifle held at waist level, covering both Judy and himself, and he brought the wagon to a halt as more Indians magically appeared. They made no sound, but were suddenly to be seen standing in places that had been unoccupied a split second before.

'Sioux,' Sieber identified the Indians aloud for himself, but Judy caught the low-spoken word.

'Is that bad?' she asked fearfully.

'No Indians are ever good news,' he told her tersely as a Sioux wearing an elaborate bear-claw necklace rode up.

The deference shown this Indian by the others was evidence enough to prove he was a chief. Younger than Sieber, the Sioux chief had a steady gaze. Sitting on his horse, he studied Sieber and Judy intently, with Sieber watching the chief while at the same time keeping an eye on the movements of one of the Sioux. A captured blue army uniform gave this Indian a ridiculous appearance, but it wasn't what the Sioux was wearing that interested Sieber, but the open interest the brave was showing in Judy.

'I am Grey Eagle,' the chief spoke, surprising Sieber with his command of English. Then he spoke in the Sioux tongue to the Indian dressed in the army uniform.

Climbing up on to the wagon, very close to Judy, the uniformed Sioux, young and sullen-faced, reached a hand for Sieber's rifle, but Sieber, in a movement that clearly showed he meant no threat, put his left hand on the weapon, holding it down on the seat.

'Every man who has tried to take something of mine has lived to regret it,' Sieber said challengingly, looking at the chief.

'Perhaps this time be different,' Grey Eagle said solemnly. 'Perhaps this time you will not live.'

'Maybe so . . . ' Sieber began, but broke off to reach out and grasp the wrist of the hand — which the uniformed Sioux was using to stroke and play with Judy's long fair hair.

She cowered back from the Indian, which permitted Sieber to position his arm so that he had a good grip on the Sioux. The Indian was strong, and for a short time both he and Sieber strained with neither making headway. Feeling the sweat oozing on to his brow, Sieber saw additional blood further darken the face of the Sioux as they both kept on the pressure.

Then Sieber, whose whole body had begun to ache, felt a slight and momentary give in the redskin's arm. It wasn't much, but it was enough to tell him that the Sioux was weakening. Using a strength he had kept in reserve, Sieber bent the Indian's arm away from him. Grunting from the effort, the Sioux tried to fight back. Sieber, a wily campaigner, suddenly eased off the pressure as if he had given up. Taken by surprise, the Sioux came off balance, and as he was thinking of pressing home the advantage he thought he had gained, Sieber wrenched his arm, throwing the Indian from the wagon to the ground.

Landing on his back, the Sioux was quick. Sieber leapt from the wagon, keeping his feet together with the intention of landing on the Indian. But the uniformed brave wasn't there. He had rolled to one side and came up on to his feet fast. When a slightly disorientated Sieber hit the ground, the Sioux was shuffling towards him at a crouch, a long-bladed knife in his hand.

Grey Eagle had dismounted to stand with his warriors, who were forming a rough circle around the two contestants the way white men did when a fight broke out on a ranch or at a mining camp.

Hearing a gasp of horror come from Judy up on the wagon, Sieber brought out his own knife, crouching a little, the knife in his right hand, left arm extended to the side to provide balance as he faced the Sioux.

The Indian made a probing jab with the knife, which Sieber easily evaded. This happened again with a kind of aimlessness to it, but then Sieber realized that each time he moved away from the Sioux he was being forced on to some uneven ground at the foot of a tree. Without a decent footing and with the tree behind him, Sieber was at a considerable disadvantage.

From the mutterings and movements going on among the spectating Sioux he gathered that they were all expecting a quick victory for their man. That was what would happen unless he swiftly worked out a strategy to defeat the uniformed Indian. Yet help unexpectedly came to Sieber. An unobserved Judy, still sitting up on the seat of the wagon, had got hold of the handle of the whip. In a rapid, sudden movement, she cracked it, whipping one of the half-dead ponies in the shafts so that it added to the distraction by squealing and struggling to get away.

With his adversary's attention distracted for an instant, Sieber jumped at him, knocking the Sioux flat on to his back. Placing a booted foot on the Indian's knife hand, Sieber pressed down until the bronzed fingers sprang open and the weapon was released to fall into the grass.

Aware that this thing had to be finished, Sieber dropped with both knees on to the chest that was covered by the scruffy army jacket, his knife hand raised ready to be slashed across the Indian's throat to sever the jugular.

That never happened. Before Sieber could bring the knife down another Sioux stepped up behind him to bring a war club down hard on to the back of Sieber's head. Immediately blacking-out, Sieber didn't hear Judy's cry of despair at what had happened to him, and he was spared her scream of alarm as two of the Sioux jumped up on to the wagon to seize her.

When he regained consciousness it was to find himself being tossed uncomfortably around. He was lying in the bed of the wagon, which was on the move. Sieber partially forgot the ache and soreness at the back of his head when he realized that his legs were trussed together from the ankles to the knees, and his hands were tied at the wrists behind his back. Lying beside him, jolting this way and that, was Judy, who was similarly bound. Raising his head a little to look out of the rear of the wagon, Sieber was incensed to see the Sioux wearing the army uniform riding his horse. The intense rage Sieber felt made his damaged head pound until it felt that it would explode. As the pain went beyond the threshold of endurance, Sieber passed out once more.

The next time he was conscious

Sieber found himself being pulled out of the wagon and dropped on to the ground. Then the Indians unceremoniously tumbled Judy from the wagon, treating her as roughly as they had him. They lay close together, and she was about to say something, her face anxious, when they were grabbed and pulled by their ankles along the rough ground, the damaged back of Sieber's head sending a burning pain knifing right through his body.

Both Judy and Sieber were put in a sitting position each against one of a pair of saplings set too far apart for them to be able to converse. They were tied firmly to the trees and then left alone. The Sioux were encamped by a river that Sieber took to be the Little Piney. Although he had never travelled that way before, he was confident that the rising of land in the distance, tall enough to lose its top in silvery clouds, was Pilot Bill. The Bozeman Trail, he told himself, was not far away.

A total absence of squaws in the

camp told Sieber that this was a raiding party. He had heard that the Sioux, brave and formidable fighters, had been harassing the army along the Bozeman Trail with hit-and-run raids made by groups of a modest size. Although the way they were moving around made it difficult to count, Sieber estimated that there were thirty Indians here.

Despite the grim situation they were in, Limm was amused to see the Sioux walking round and round the rickety old wagon, touching it, stroking it, making comments. The wagon was likely to fall apart the next time it moved, but the Indians were inspecting and admiring it the way he had seen farmers examine a gleaming new machine. The only thing of value was Traynor's saddle, which was still in the wagon. Conversely, as they used no more than a blanket on the back of a horse, the Sioux had no interest in the saddle.

They moved away from the wagon then, and began smearing paint on their own bodies and then coating their horses with it. Conscious of the watching Judy's alarm, sensing that she saw this strange scene as being of danger to them, he regretted not being able to explain to her what was happening, but he could only do so by shouting, and that might prove dangerous by exciting the Sioux.

The colouring the Indians were using on themselves and the horses was sacred medicine paint. This told Sieber that they were going out on a raid. What would that mean for Judy and himself? He was pondering on what the Indians' intentions towards them might be, when Grey Eagle walked slowly over to stand looking down at him, his face grave.

'We wanted only peace, but the soldiers steal our hunting grounds, so Red Cloud has told the White Chief that there must be war,' the Indian said, slowly and thoughtfully.

'We are not soldiers,' Sieber pointed out, using what little movement his bonds would permit to include Judy in his protest.

Drawing his blanket more tightly around him, the Sioux chief delayed answering, then he said, 'That is so, but you should have stayed back on the far side of Powder River. It is not for me to ask why you come here. You are on our land in a time of war.'

'What will you do with us?' Sieber asked.

Looking at Sieber for a long time, face impassive although Sieber felt he could read regret in it, the chief suddenly turned his back on him, signalled to his waiting warriors, and walked slowly away as the braves started up a war chant.

It went on and on, a repetitive, monotonous chanting that seeped into the heads of the two bound white people, unnerving both of them, Sieber because he was aware of his own helplessness. It was cool, but he could see the beads of sweat on Judy's brow, and fear was bringing a twitch to the side of her mouth as she watched the Indians become excited, reeling like drunken men before falling into the regular, short, rhythmic steps of a war dance.

With the chanting changing pitch, the dance continued, seemingly endless. Accepting that there was no immediate threat to Judy and himself, Sieber felt sorry for whoever the Siouxs' target was. He thought it likely that it would be a patrol of soldiers, perhaps a lone wood train with an inadequate escort because of the demands being made of the army out here. He could imagine how the Indians would strike, swiftly and unexpectedly, hatred for the white man and the cause of protecting their hunting grounds making them ruthless.

The dance ended at last, and Grey Eagle led his warriors in mounting up on swift ponies. They rode out with not one of them glancing back at the two white captives. But they left behind three braves to guard Judy and Sieber.

They squatted by a small fire, eating. All three kept a keen watch on the two prisoners, but one, sullen-faced and menacing, hardly took his eyes off Sieber for a moment.

It was the Sioux wearing an army uniform. Sieber was under no illusion. With that particular Sioux left behind, then Sieber would not live to see the return of the party of Indians. His only hope was that the resentful Sioux would seek vengeance only against him, and would spare Judy.

5

The raid had not come as a surprise. In the three days of solid rain since they had brought the herd along the trail from Fort Reno, the horizons on all sides had at no time been free of furtively moving Sioux scouts. When they had been without rain for a full twenty-four hours, Joe McGlory believed an attack by Indians to be inevitable. Anticipating it was a hindrance, for he had made great progress in shaping his men into a body as disciplined as any army unit, and every bit as reliable. McGlory had appointed Matthew Grady, an experienced cowpuncher who had none of the bandy-legged awkwardness that made many a cowboy useless out of the saddle, as trail boss. Observing Grady secretly for some time, McGlory was convinced that he was a man who could handle himself, and a gun, in any situation. His confidence was justified, for when the Sioux did come, boiling up over a hill to charge down with shouts of '*Hoka hey!*' Grady had proved himself in the skirmish that had followed.

With the attack over in a short time, it was the aftermath that was causing Joe McGlory problems. One man, a boy name Johnny Wells, needed to have an arrow removed from his shoulder, while old Will Fermoy had sustained a head injury from a bullet that ripped away the upper part of his right ear.

The Sioux had cut away a good slice of the herd, and the remaining longhorns had stampeded. With Kitty safe back with the chuckwagon, McGlory and Grady had ridden with the hands toward the head of the stampede to break the flight. In a riot of bellowing cattle, revolvers fired to turn the lead animals, and clouds of choking dust, they succeeded first in forcing the herd into a great milling circle, and then getting the cattle back under control.

'We've lost Charlie Weldon some-wheres,' Matt Grady pulled his bandanna down from his face to shout a report to McGlory.

Weldon was the horse wrangler, the job usually taken on by youngsters eager to move up to being a cowhand. Charlie, a little fellow who was full of fun and ready to work hard, had joined in the fight to control the herd without being asked. A stampede was a dangerous thing for an inexperienced rider, and McGlory feared the worst.

'I'll go look for him, Joe. You carry on here,' Kitty called, about to mount up when Joe called sharply to her.

'No!' McGlory shouted. His wife had no idea what she might find in the wake of a stampede, and he wanted to spare her. 'Grady and me'll go.'

The light was fading and dusk was moving in on them as they rode past the now placid but well guarded herd. Both men rode with heads down, eyes scanning the ground; both hoping for the best but fearing the worst. It was McGlory who made the first discovery, the ribs of a horse, scraped bare of hide.

'Matt!' he called tersely.

Dismounting, holding the reins of their horses, they walked slowly in small circles that they widened at each turn, coming together when a circle had been completed. In that way they found what was left of Charlie Weldon. He had been trampled, mashed into the ground with the rest of his horse, flesh and bones pounded as flat as a pancake.

'Reckon as how Charlie's going to have to be scraped up, not lifted up,' Grady observed calmly.

'Come on,' McGlory said, mounting up.

They rode back to where most of the hands stood waiting with Kitty by the chuckwagon. Dismounting with his horse still on the move, McGlory strode to the chuckwagon. Bending, he pulled the spade from beneath it and tossed it like a spear through the failing light at Clancy Magee, who caught the tool with one hand, but had an expression of uncertainty on his face.

'You'll find Charlie Weldon out there. Bury him,' McGlory said.

'You a-going to read a few words from the Bible over him, boss?' Magee enquired, adding, 'It's customary.'

'In the morning,' McGlory replied, unconcern in his tone, but then his voice and his manner sharpened when he said, 'Tonight we have work to do. I intend to track down those hostiles and get my beef back. Now hear me good. I'm not going to press any man here to join me, but those who will, step forward.'

He gave a nod of satisfaction as the cowboys took one step forwards to a man. 'Fine. Now fetch your Remingtons, men. We ride out in five minutes.'

As McGlory went to get his own rifle and some boxes of shells, Kitty moved in close to his side, morose-sounding as she said, 'That boy is our first death, Joe. Could it be a bad omen?'

He loaded the Remington, the metallic clicking of shells loud on the evening air. 'There'll be more deaths between now and sun-up, Kitty, but that isn't a bad omen because I'll have our cattle back.'

'I hope that you're right about the cattle, Joe. Please take care.'

McGlory left her without a word, only the chinking of his spurs bidding her farewell as he walked to his horse and where the mounted men waited, made indistinct by twilight.

With the sun gone from it the air was cold as they rode at a steady pace. The light was going fast and the shadows advanced creepily from the lowlands. The high rise of Pilot Hill to their right still glowed with a faint crimson as it courted the last rays of a departing sun. Soon it would become a silhouetted landmark that would be invaluable through the night.

With no one speaking and with McGlory and Grady riding together at the head, the column of nineteen men rode up and down hills. Then they were in a dry-bottomed gulch, a canopy of stars overhead and a brooding silence all around that was broken unobtrusively by the sound of horses' hooves on the soft ground. A background of infinitely faint sound came from the movement of brushwood that was pushed aside by the chap-covered legs of the riders as they passed.

They rode between a few juniper trees to come out on to the plain. Now the eerie stillness had gone, to be replaced by a high moaning wind. Carried on this wind, moving over a long distance through the thin air of night, came the bawling of a cow.

McGlory and Grady exchanged glances, and there was a close to imperceptible ripple of anticipation that affected the men behind them. The sound was reassurance that they were heading in the right direction. It had been easy to follow the trail of the Sioux, who hadn't bothered to cover their tracks or try to lead their pursuers astray, for it would be pointless due to the unmistakable signs left by the stolen herd of cattle.

Going up a modest rise that ascended in three levels, McGlory held up a hand to bring his men to a halt as he and Grady reined up on the upper rim. Ahead of them, lying flat and peaceful was the Sioux encampment. The cattle stolen from the McGlory trail herd were standing as still as a gigantic tableau, the tepees of the Indians erected round them to form a corral of sorts. Even from a distance, McGlory could see the embers of a fire that was under a cut-bank to protect it from the stiff winds that were blowing on this cold night.

McGlory was undecided about what to do next. The Indians, apparently confident that they hadn't been followed, nor did they expect to be, had posted no sentinels, no look-outs. But in front of McGlory and his men was a gradual slope scattered with loose stones. This meant that the horses would make a loud rattling noise in the night that would lose them the element of surprise before they hit the camp, regardless of how fast they rode.

But to make a detour would take up too much time, and tire both the men and the horses. McGlory concluded that, deprived of the chance to surprise the Sioux, creating confusion among them would be the second-best strategy. Turning in the saddle, he addressed his men in a tone that, though low, carried clearly to the riders at the back.

'We are going to split up and hit them from both sides. You men who are behind Matt now, you follow him. Matt, you ride to the left. Take that bright star yonder as a marker. Ride towards it. I'll be riding in on the right with the rest of the men. Keep going at the star until you hear me fire two quick shots, one right after the other.

That will be the signal to turn towards the camp.'

Facing forward again in his saddle, McGlory then said a few final words. 'When we hit them, we hit them hard! Go in for the kill. Don't leave one red-skin alive. The cattle will scatter, but we'll round them up afterwards.'

They sat in silence for a while, each man lost in his own thoughts, each wondering what sort of a fight lay up ahead. Joe McGlory concentrated on the plan to get back his stolen beef. Although not a religious man, he was becoming increasingly aware of his continuing good fortune in life. It was happening in a way that suggested to him that he was being looked after by some benevolent god.

Avenging his sister had made him an outlaw, but Joe had seen that as a small price to pay for punishing those who had abused and murdered her. Then he had met Kitty, and it was her ingenuity that had not only saved him from the gallows but had freed him from the stigma and burden of Apache Joe, while giving him a new life as Joe McGlory. His new identity was safe and secure because Apache Joe was officially dead. Having this second chance in life, together with Kitty as a wife, made Joe determined to succeed in this cattle drive.

Losing his identity in circumstances that could have it construed as emasculation because he had taken his wife's name didn't worry Joe in the slightest. He had never known who he actually was. His sister who had been killed, and another sister and two brothers still at the San Carlos reservation, were definitely Apaches, but Joe had always been different. The Apaches, old and young, male and female, had accepted him as one of them, but Joe had always been aware of an inner sense of alienation. As a boy he had asked his Apache 'father', Man-Who-Makes-Thunder, why, particularly where the colour of skin was concerned, he was not the same as those around him.

For some reason the question had saddened the old Apache chief, who had promised Joe that when he was a few years older he would be told his history. When Joe had mentioned this to his mother, a squaw who put her family first in all things, but was too remote from them to be loved, she had replied that she and the older Apaches knew the story but were sworn to keep the secret. Only Man-Who-Makes-Thunder could tell Joe the truth.

When Joe had been fourteen years old, an especially hard winter brought about the death of Man-Who-Makes-Thunder. The older Apaches who had been predeceased by Joe's 'father' had since then refused to give him an answer to the mystery that bothered him greatly.

Pushing all that from his mind now, he muttered, 'Move,' as he dug in his spurs. His horse leapt forwards, only slightly ahead of that of Grady, and they went sliding, slithering and hoof-rattling through the shale. Then they were parting, two columns dividing from the front, first making a 'V' and then becoming completely disconnected as the distance between them grew.

First aware of the cattle among the tepees becoming startled into restlessness, McGlory then saw the Sioux scrambling out of their tepees. He kept pressing on hard, froth from the mouth and nostrils of his galloping horse blowing back at him. From the thundering of hoofs close behind he knew that his cowboys were staying with him. Watching to his left, measuring carefully to find a point ahead when he would be level with the Sioux encampment, McGlory pulled his rifle from its scabbard and pointed it at the sky, butt resting on his right thigh. Judging it right, he fired off two rapid shots, then wheeled his horse sharply to the left.

His men, seasoned westerners, wheeled with him. Without being told they abandoned the single file column and fanned out so they were riding in a line side-by-side towards the camp, with McGlory on the far end of that line. Mentally praising them for their spontaneous and natural fighting manoeuvre, he saw them drawing their Remingtons as they galloped headlong at the Sioux.

The firing began then. An Indian, bare to the waist, long hair swinging wildly, came out of a tepee on all fours. Armed only with a bow, he came upright and pulled back with his left arm as he aimed an arrow in McGlory's direction. McGlory fired, the bow fell sideways out of the hands of the Sioux, the arrow going off harmlessly to McGlory's right as the Indian did a leap high into the air, impelled by some dying reaction in his nervous system. The Sioux seemed to remain suspended in the air, but then he fell to earth, doing the unmistakable flopping drop of a dead body.

Caught in a crossfire between

McGlory's men and Grady's column, the Sioux were panicking and dying because of it. McGlory and his cowboys had brought down at least nine Indians without serious retaliation. Then they were in among the tepees, using the rifle stocks to club down Indians who were trying to flee but had nowhere to go. Those Sioux still alive when they fell, died under the slashing, cutting, mashing hoofs of the cowboys as they jerked their horses this way and that. Rounding a tepee, McGlory had to pull on the reins so hard that his horse reared up on its back legs. Standing in front of him, face impassive, arms folded, his very stance a challenge, was a Sioux.

There were several options open to McGlory. With his rifle he could easily have shot the Indian from the saddle, or he could have ridden by, smashing his head in with the stock. McGlory could have ridden at the Sioux, letting the horse knock down and mash the Indian into the ground. But he did none of those things.

With the sounds of what amounted to a massacre of the Indians going on around him, McGlory dismounted and walked to face the Sioux, who pointed a finger at the rifle McGlory was carrying. Telling himself that he had been foolish to get off his horse, McGlory then did something more stupid by walking back to the animal and replacing the rifle in its scabbard. When he faced the Indian again he wore his gunbelt with its holstered .38, while the only other weapon he carried was a knife sheathed at his waist. The Sioux standing before him had no gun, but a knife with a double-edged blade thrust into a band worn round his midriff.

'I am Grey Eagle,' the Sioux said, raising his voice above the mayhem going on nearby. 'Why do you wish to kill my people?'

'Why did you steal my cattle, Chief?' McGlory retaliated.

'Through all time the Sioux have

pitched their tepees along these streams. We were as free as any people have ever been, bound only by the earth and sky. These hunting grounds were sacred, the bison and the elk, our food, our clothing, our shelter, were sacred animals. You tell me why white men steal our buffalo.'

The logic of this had McGlory stymied. He said, 'I guess you've got the better of me there, Chief. But what are you and me doing? The two of us can't put everything to rights.'

'You speak true. Now it is too late for Grey Eagle,' the Sioux chief said solemnly.

'What are you saying we should do, Chief Grey Eagle?' McGlory enquired, respecting this brave Indian who could have run and saved his life, but had chosen to stay and face the leader of the men slaughtering his people.

'It is your decision,' the Sioux replied, using a nod to indicate McGlory's six-shooter. 'You can shoot me down like a dog, the way your warriors are killing my people, or you can permit me to die with honour and dignity. Let it be a fight to the death.'

It was a challenge that united with memories from McGlory's boyhood days with the Apaches. His mind was filled with the primitive appeal of it, one man against the other, honour in victory for one, dignity in death for the other. The prospect of such combat sent a surge through McGlory so powerful that he lost all sense of responsibility to Kitty and the cattle drive. All that belonged in a different world to the savage world that this Sioux chief had enticed him into.

The shooting, the shouting and shrieking, the thudding of hooves was abating now. This meant, McGlory knew, that few, if any, Sioux remained alive. Unbuckling his gunbelt he laid it in the grass, beckoning Grey Eagle to follow him as he walked away from the chance of his men finding him. They went down close to the river, where the night sky reflected off the water to give them more light for their contest.

'I should go to tell my men that if you win you are to go free, Grey Eagle.'

Looking at McGlory for a long moment, the Sioux said firmly, 'No, if I beat you, then let them kill me. Living holds nothing for Grey Eagle now.'

This statement went deep in McGlory. He was in a fight to the death with an opponent who wanted to die regardless of the outcome. This knowledge didn't frighten McGlory, but it did tell him that a formidable struggle lay ahead.

Taking his knife from behind the sash, Grey Eagle unnecessarily tested both edges of the blade for sharpness by running a thumb along them. In a quiet, friendly manner, he asked, 'Who are you, white man?'

'Apache Joe,' McGlory announced automatically, the years of semi-civilization and restraint since he had become Joe McGlory now never having seemed to have existed.

'I have heard of you,' the Sioux said,

looking relaxed and content for the first time since Joe had come upon him. For a fraction of a second it would have been possible to believe that Grey Eagle was about to smile. Then the Indian continued to speak. 'If you should beat me, Apache Joe, then I will die a very proud man.'

Both holding knives in their right hands, they reached out with their left hands to touch, a kind of warriors' handshake, and then they were circling each other warily. Voices reached them from across the short distance from the camp. McGlory could hear his men asking questions, giving each other some answers, and he assumed that they were searching for him. Finding his horse would baffle them.

Fast and accurate, Grey Eagle slashed at McGlory, aiming for the tendons between the fore and upper parts of the right arm, intending to disable him. So fast was the Indian that McGlory couldn't completely avoid the short sideways movement of the knife. The tip cut through his coat and shirt sleeves, slicing the skin as it went by, drawing blood but doing no serious damage.

In fact the injury increased the thrill of combat for McGlory. All the self-discipline he had employed since leaving the renegade trail now ebbed away. At that moment the lightness of his skin and the doubts about his ancestry didn't matter. He was what he had been up to the time of meeting Kitty McGlory, he was an Apache.

When Grey Eagle lunged again, McGlory parried and their knife hands locked together up high. With their bodies tight against each other, the Sioux kneed McGlory cruelly in the groin. Close to being disabled by the agony that had his body in its grip, McGlory fought away the fog that was trying to fill his head and threatened to weaken him so that he would no longer hold off Grey Eagle's knife hand.

Feeling the Indian's body movements, McGlory was aware that the Sioux was about to knee him again, and knew that he couldn't withstand the pain of a second such attack. Reaching with his left hand, McGlory got a grip of the bear-claw necklace for leverage. McGlory swung up his left elbow to smash it into the Indian's face.

It was a heavy enough blow to send the Sioux staggering backwards, and McGlory went after him, going for Grey Eagle's stomach with his knife. Feeling the blade go in to the hilt, McGlory braced himself to drag it sideways to finish the Sioux off, but the Indian either stumbled back or took evasive action, for McGory's bloody knife came free.

But Grey Eagle was badly injured. He faced McGlory again, knife held at the ready, but he was bending over, trying to hold his ripped-open belly together with his left hand. Yet the Sioux was full of courage and had amazing strength. Once more their knife hands became locked at arm's length above their heads. This time

Grey Eagle seemed about to collapse. He was falling away from McGlory, although their knives were still joined. But the chief was a cunning fighter, as McGlory was about to discover when the Sioux fell on his back but kept hold of McGlory, placed both moccasined feet in his belly and threw him in a somersault so that he went over the top of the Indian to land heavily on his face in the stinking, marshy edge of the river.

Frightened water rats scurried away, one of them scratching McGlory's face as it scrambled over him, the reek of its wet, greasy fur foul. Then he had no more time to worry about rats. Grey Eagle was on him, turning him face down, knees on his back, pushing him down into the water.

Unable to breathe, McGlory bucked and jolted like a half-broken bronco as he unsuccessfully tried to dislodge the Sioux. Lungs bursting, brain seeming to swell inside his head so that it felt in danger of exploding, McGlory threshed about helplessly in the water. Then by luck his left hand once again found the elaborate necklace. Yanking down hard, McGlory pulled the Indian's face down into the water so that it smacked hard against the back of his head. With an effort he was able to roll Grey Eagle off his back, but McGlory couldn't surface quick enough and his lungs half filled with water.

Standing, knee-deep in the river, bent over as he coughed, choked and retched, McGlory struggled to regain the ability to breathe as he saw Grey Eagle coming up out of the water. Initially believing that the Sioux had lost his knife, McGlory then saw the blade glint dully in the poor light of night. The fight was to go on, and Grey Eagle was the toughest man he had ever faced. Still clearing water from his lungs, with difficulty, McGlory lacked the strength to fight on for much longer, and, to his surprise, found the will for combat start to slip from him.

Determined to gain the advantage,

desperately needing to do so, McGlory stumbled up out of the water on to the bank. But the Sioux had beaten him to it. A little further along the bank, Grey Eagle was shaking himself like a dog, freeing himself of as much water as possible, before he came at a run for McGlory.

Brain working fast, understanding that to prolong this contest of skill and strength would result in the death of both of them, McGlory worked out a plan. He stayed standing, knife held out as the Indian charged at him. But when Grey Eagle was no more than two feet away, and was driving his knife forwards and upwards at McGlory's chest, McGlory dropped to his right. Hitting the ground, he swung himself quickly round and slashed with his knife as the Sioux passed by. The knife cut deeply across the back of both of the Indian's knees, and he dropped like a shot buffalo. McGlory was on him, straddling the Sioux, making sure of the kill as he rammed his knife home between Grey Eagle's ribs and right on through into his heart.

Exhausted, McGlory fell sideways off the Indian. Then the most amazing thing happened. Grey Eagle got up, very unsteadily. Wobbling a few steps on legs that wouldn't work because they had been half severed at the knees, he toppled over into the river. Kneeling up, McGlory watched the water around the corpse darken with blood as the river took his erst-while adversary away from him forever.

A short while later, able to breathe fairly normally again, McGlory got shakily to his feet. He felt a sadness over the death of a worthy opponent, but some kind of throw-back to his younger days promoted an immense exhilaration in him at having been victorious in bloody hand-to-hand combat. On impulse and without regard to the consequences, McGlory threw back his head and released a ringing Apache war cry.

From not far away in the night he

heard a trembling voice ask, 'What in tarnation was that?'

'A redskin we missed,' another voice complained.

Recognizing the voices as those of his own men, McGlory, not realizing the danger he was in, walked through the darkness to them.

'There he is! Shoot the varmint!' a man cried out and there came the solid clicking of a Remington rifle bolt.

Then came a crack of a rifle shot, and a bullet whistled closely by McGlory's head, causing him to shout.

'Hold it, that's Joe,' he heard Matt Grady say.

'That ain't McGlory,' a cowpuncher argued. 'He was hollering like a loco redskin.'

'I said hold it,' Grady sternly warned, coming out of the night to meet McGlory. 'What happened to you, Joe?'

'Ran into a bit of trouble,' McGlory replied, realizing for the first time that his clothing was wet through from the river and stained with blood, Grey Eagle's and his own.

'We found the Sioux had a couple of prisoners, Joe. A man and a woman, both white,' Grady said, guiding McGlory to where a man and a woman stood in the shadows.

Walking up, McGlory found himself looking at Limm Sieber, who said with the emphasis of a man solving a hundreds-of-years-old riddle, 'I knew you weren't dead.'

There was surprise on the pretty face of the woman next to Sieber, and she looked from him to McGlory and back again. Staring into Sieber's eyes, conscious of the animosity glaring back at him, McGlory gritted, 'There can't be any reason for me not to kill you right here and now.'

There was a grunting of surprise from McGlory's men as they heard this, and the woman took one fearful step forward, checking herself, standing staring at the two men who stood close, face to face, their stances threatening.

'I guess you have no option but to kill me,' Sieber replied in a low, steady voice. 'If you don't, then I'll make sure you end up dangling on the end of a rope.'

'You two know each other?' Grady asked superfluously, a frown on his weatherbeaten face.

'I guess I know him a whole lot better than you do,' Sieber said.

The threat in Sieber's tone had Grady cover him, and the hands standing around brought up their rifles.

'What do we do, Joe?' Grady asked.

Pausing for a moment, McGlory said, 'Bring them along. Make sure that the woman's fixed up comfortable.'

6

'I did my durned best, boss,' Magee the cook excused himself to McGlory, after complaining that he had broken the handle of the shovel, that the ground was hard, and that he could do no more for Charlie Weldon than to scrape a hollow underneath him, line it with the young wrangler's horse blanket, and tip the pulped mess of a corpse into it. Magee had then completed the grave by piling round smooth rocks on top.

McGlory, standing higher on the hillside than the others, an open Bible in his hands, looked down uncomfortably at his wife and his men, who had formed up as mourners. Sieber was there, too, looking up at him, the woman, made more disturbingly attractive by the way she seemed to have taken a step away from life, at his side.

This wasn't McGlory's kind of scene. A knife or a gun suited his hand much better than the Holy Book. The fight with Grey Eagle had badly unsettled him. In the hours since it had happened his ambition to be a good husband to Kitty and a successful businessman was being eroded by a call of the wild, an awakening of the savage that had lain less than semi-dormant in him. He and Limm Sieber hadn't spoken, but there was no need for words between them. Both were aware that Sieber was committed to capturing him for the law, and McGlory was equally as resolute in preventing that from happening.

All of the cattle taken by the Sioux had been rounded up and returned to the herd. All was well, or should have been well, but McGlory knew that Kitty had noticed that he had changed while out after the Indians, and that this worried her. He was confident that he would recover from what was a reminder of what total freedom, the art of living to the full, was like. It certainly had more appeal than the life of constraint he had been trying, successfully, to adapt to. It would take time, he knew that, but McGlory promised himself that he would eventually become what Kitty wanted him to be. What she had a right to expect him to be, as he would be nothing but a hanged criminal had it not been for her.

McGlory looked down at the clumsily constructed grave, hoping the sight of it would put him in the right condition for reading from the Bible. Magee, seeing McGlory looking at the grave, put the wrong construction on what he saw.

'I couldn't do no better without proper tools,' the cook shouted up at McGlory.

'No one's blaming you for anything, Clancy,' Grady reprimanded the cook. 'Now shut it, and let Joe get on.'

Leafing through the Bible, McGlory felt the chill that was in the air, and was concerned. It was imperative that they got the herd to Montana before the first snows fell, and time was getting short. The words on the pages in his hands blurred as he frantically studied them for something that could fittingly be read. There was nothing that he could find. Closing his eyes for a moment he recalled something his Apache 'father' had once recited to him. The words had fixed themselves inside Joe McGlory's head, and he repeated them now, hearing his own voice hollowly reverberate.

It is one and the same thing
to be living or dead, or awake,
or asleep, young or old. The
former aspect in each case
becomes the latter, and the latter
again the former, by sudden unexpected
reversal.

There was a silence of astonishment at the depth of McGlory's words, and then there was a muttered, raggedy chorus of 'Amens' that didn't seem to fit in with what he had said over the grave.

'You never fail to amaze me, Joe,' Kitty commented, proud of him when he came down the hillside to join her. Then her smile died, and she asked him worriedly. 'What of Sieber?'

This was a question that McGlory had been asking himself ever since he had come upon the bounty hunter out in the night. Sieber was a real problem, that was beyond dispute. He was a hard man, a determined man. There was only one way to stop a man of Sieber's calibre, and it was clear to McGlory that there would have to be a showdown between himself and the bounty hunter, who was at that moment advancing on them, Judy lightly holding his arm.

'Begging your pardon, Miss Kitty,' Sieber said, politely touching the brim of his stetson, 'but I was hoping that you might let Judy ride in the buggy with you.'

The two women looked uncertainly

at each other; one red-haired, feisty and confident, the other withdrawn, so battered by life that recovery didn't seem likely. Judy tried a beginning smile, and Kitty responded with a welcoming smile of her own.

'Of course you must ride with me, Judy,' Kitty said, putting an arm round the other woman's shoulders and taking her to the buggy.

As Sieber walked away, McGlory went after him. They stopped not far from the chuckwagon, where only Clancy Magee might overhear if he should stop rattling his pots and pans, but they would know when that happened.

'What have you in mind, Sieber?' McGlory asked.

'About you, Apache Joe?'

Nodding, McGlory said, 'It was all a very long time ago.'

'I never forget, Joe, no matter how much time passes,' Sieber said quietly. 'If I tried to in your case, then the fact that another man was found dead in your place would stop me. An innocent man died to save your neck, Apache Joe.'

'Innocent . . . ?' McGlory seemed about to protest, but then he asked a question. 'Do you want to settle it here and now?'

'No,' Sieber shook his head. 'This drive is important to Kitty, and these cowboys have already risked their lives, and will do so again. No, Apache Joe, you finish the drive. But remember that once we're in Montana I'll come for you.'

'I'll be ready,' McGlory told him, then turned on his heel to walk away, anxious to move along the Bozeman Trail again, with Fort Phil Kearney as the next stop.

★ ★ ★

They reached the fort without incident. Sieber had earned his keep by riding drag, and he was one of the first shift of cowboys McGlory permitted to go into the fort while the others stayed minding the herd.

Built on the River Piney, Fort Phil Kearney was far from finished when Sieber paid his visit, taking Judy with him. The thick, loophole walls were complete, but few wooden buildings had been constructed, and regular lines of tents had been pitched to serve in the meantime. The fort, commanded by Colonel Henry B. Carrington, was under strict discipline that was extended to civilians as well as military personnel.

Music and the various sounds made by men drinking came from a huge tent and Sieber, with a hand on Judy's arm, walked to it and they went in. At first the sight inside the tent was in such contrast to the regimentation in the remainder of the fort that it was difficult to believe it was real. A male pianist hammered at the keys as he played and sang 'Where Was Moses When the Light Went Out'. Soldiers and civilians drank, joined in the singing, played cards, and argued. There were women there, too, bawdy saloon girls, most of them in some stage of intoxication. Looking around, Sieber could see just about every type of male on the human scale, right from the good to the bad. Bored young soldiers were drinking themselves into a temporary escape from military discipline, cowboys were relaxing after long days on the trail, while those of nefarious profession stood around, their hard eyes looking for any opportunity that might present itself.

'Life goes on,' Judy said in her low voice, her words without emphasis so that Sieber couldn't decipher her meaning.

This wasn't the kind of place that he would choose to take her, but he had no choice where entertainment was concerned in Fort Phil Kearney. Judy and himself had become as close as it is possible for two people who give neither nothing of their pasts nor nothing of themselves. Able to tell that she welcomed the protection he afforded her, he was also able to sense that his hard-man characteristics and six-gun frightened her more than a little. Although Judy was aware of there being something serious between him and Apache Joe, she didn't know what it was. Kitty and Judy, two women coming together in a wilderness peopled by men, were enjoying each other's company. Judy had lost a lot of her reticence since finding friendship with Kitty. Would she, Sieber wondered, get around to asking Joe's wife what his interest in Joe was, and if she did, what would Kitty tell her?

A little man with a high white collar that held his head rigidly, jumped up on the small stage, gave the pianist a friendly slap on the back, then made a shouted announcement.

'Now, for your pleasure and entertainment, ladies and gentlemen,' said the little man, who had a rat face and an English accent, 'Miss Fanny

Montmorency will sing 'Love Among the Roses'.'

'Miss Fanny Montmorency is a whore!' a man shouted from the crowd.

'Nevertheless,' the rat-faced man continued without either faltering or glancing in the direction of the heckler, 'Miss Fanny Montmorency will now sing 'Love Among the Roses'.'

A well-fleshed woman stepped up on to the stage her bosom bulging over the top of her dress, to the delight of the male drinkers who shouted and cheered. But then even they fell quiet as the woman began to sing in an unexpectedly sweet and melodious way. Judy, facing Sieber as they both stood with an elbow on the counter, closed her eyes and swayed her head to the beat of the song. Aware that she had retreated into a world of memories where there was no place for him, Sieber found himself idly listening to a one-way conversation going on behind him. Then he suddenly became interested as he heard a man speaking in a moderately boastful manner.

'The rope I use is a neatly worked one,' the voice was saying. 'I carry it in this little black satchel, see? I can slip it over the head of a culprit with such dexterity that he hardly notices. Not only do I avoid giving distress and needless pain, but I also intone a few well-timed words of such fine sympathy that they inspire confidence in the victim himself. I have here the black cap that I slip over their heads. Would you care to see it?'

Turning, Sieber saw a portly, intense young fellow talking to a soldier who was agog. As the man pulled a black hood from a satchel, Sieber asked, 'Is your name William?'

'Indeed it is, my good sir.'

'Could I have seen you down south?' Sieber enquired.

'That you may well have done, sir, for I travel far and wide,' William replied. 'My services cost just one hundred dollars, cheap at the price, even if I say so myself.' William gave an apologetic little giggle. 'I am presently proceeding to Virginia City, where my thoroughness and efficiency are required to dispense with a culprit named Silas Morgan, who burned an hotel to the ground.'

Miss Fanny Montmorency had finished her song and, whore or not, the applause she received was so enthusiastically tumultuous that Sieber had to delay his last question. Then he asked. 'Could it be that I saw you where a renegade named Apache Joe was to be hanged?'

'A bad business that,' William said dolefully. 'I had the scaffold built, everything working as smoothly as a rattler sliding downhill. Cheated, I was, cheated more cruelly than any man should be in this world.'

'The law was cheated,' Sieber remarked. 'Somebody did well to get a dead body in past Sheriff Comber.'

William held off his reply, partly because of the noise as a small orchestra that had taken the stage struck up and a quadrille began, partly because he was watching girls dance, gliding through the figures with genuine grace. Hanging might be William's principal interest, Sieber mused wryly, but it didn't seem to be his only one. Then Sieber was stunned by what the hangman said next.

'Correction, my good sir,' William said with a smile to excuse him putting the tough Sieber right. 'That man was not dead. He walked into that jail as alive as you and me are right this very minute.'

'Then he was murdered in there!' an astounded Sieber said. 'You were there, William. You must have been a part of that plot.'

His upset showing on his face, William protested. 'Nay, my good sir, nay, indeed. I am no felon. You speak to the man who has been the master of ceremonies at the execution of many a famous wrongdoer. I cannot answer your questions about that affair, but would suggest that you address them to the Reverend Lionel Anthom, a veritable man of God.'

'To use one of your turns of phrase, William,' Sieber said dully, 'that would be like looking for that needle in a haystack.'

'Indeed not, my good sir. I am travelling to Virginia City with Mr Anthom, who is here at this very minute, in this very fort.'

★ ★ ★

Joe and Kitty McGlory were walking beside the grass that had been roughly cut to make a parade ground. Wood-choppers filled the air with clumping thuds as they laboured at shaping timber up for the construction of badly needed buildings. On their way to see the commanding officer, the McGlorys wanted to get their horses shod, their supplies replenished, and be back on the trail as swiftly as possible. Within no more than a week it was likely that

150

blizzards would be raging. Any long delay here at the fort would certainly cause them additional problems, and might even prevent them from reaching Montana. Getting snowed in on the Bozeman Trail was a prospect that was too daunting even to contemplate. If they personally were to be able to survive such a winter, it would be to see their herd and their dreams perish.

Further over to the left of the parade ground a group of civilians and off-duty soldiers stood with their backs to the McGlorys. The crowd was listening to a man standing on something that the McGlorys couldn't see, but as the orator's words, distorted by distance, reached them, Joe stopped Kitty by placing a hand on her arm.

'Do you hear what I hear?' an incredulous McGlory asked, and they both listened.

'In this Christian age,
'Tis strange you'll engage,
When everything's doing high

crimes to assauge,
That direst offences continue to
rage;
That fibbing and fobbing,
And thieving and robbing,
The foulest maltreating,
And forging and lifting,
And wickedly shifting
The goods that belong to another
away
Are the dark misdemeanors of
every day.'

'That has to be Lionel Anthom!'
Kitty looked bewildered. 'What can he
be doing here?'

'Preaching in verse, as always,'
McGlory grinned. 'Come on, Kit,
we'll see the colonel first and then
say howdy to the reverend.'

But when they reached the head-
quarter company office it was to find
Colonel Carrington absent. As they
entered a building that was so new
that an aroma of resin was heavy on
the air, it was Captain Flynn, who

was just as surprised as they were, who stood up from behind a desk to shake hands with them.

'We didn't expect to see you here, Captain Flynn,' McGlory said.

'It came as something of a shock to me to be made adjutant here at Phil Kearney,' Flynn said, adding ruefully, 'I am more than pleased to see both of you. I am glad that my warning to you was inaccurate.'

'So far,' McGlory agreed, in the knowledge that they were facing more hazards than there were behind them.

'Mrs Flynn?' Kitty enquired. 'Is she here with you?'

'She is not, thank the Lord. Life is not easy back at Fort Laramie, Mrs McGlory, but it is positively perilous here,' Captain Flynn said.

From outside came the clash of cymbals and a flaring of trumpets as a military band began to play. On hearing the stirring music, Flynn, young, moustachioed and handsome, every inch a soldier, walked slowly to the window and looked out.

He turned his head to the McGlorys to say, 'There was a time, not long ago I confess, when the sound of that band filled me with pride.'

'And now?' McGlory asked quietly.

'Now . . . ' The captain seemed unsure whether to speak what was on his mind. Then he went on, 'Now, McGlory, it fills me with fear. Don't misunderstand me, for it is not the personal fear of a coward that afflicts me. It is fear for my men, for my fellow officers, a fear brought on by military intelligence that has me know what is out there.'

'That bad, Captain?' a frowning Kitty enquired.

Flynn nodded. 'Red Cloud has just about all the Sioux bands out there ready to attack — his Oglalas, the Hunkpapas, Miniconjous, Gros Ventres, Cheyennes, and Arapahoes.' The captain lowered his voice, throwing a cautious look towards the closed door before he continued, 'I will

154

countermand my earlier advice to you, McGlory, Mrs McGlory. Colonel Carrington will suggest that you remain here at the fort for safety. It is my considered opinion that you would be at less risk to face whatever may await you out on the trail.'

'Thank you, Captain . . . ' Kitty was saying when the door opened and Colonel Henry B. Carrington marched smartly in.

A brusque man with a clipped moustache, the colonel barely acknowledged the introductions made by Flynn. As if it was a foregone conclusion, he said to McGlory, 'As you will have seen, this fort is in a continued state of emergency. In addition to the necessity of keeping my troops on alert, I have to oversee the completion of warehouses, stockades and quarters ready for winter. Having regard to this situation, McGlory, I trust that you have abandoned all plans to move on north.'

'On the contrary, sir,' McGlory

answered, 'I am planning to move out before noon tomorrow.'

Disgust at such a naive plan registered on the colonel's red face. Grasping McGlory's shoulder he moved him towards the door, opening it, stepping out and pulling McGlory out with him, pointing to a high ridge in the middle distance. It was dwarfed by the Big Horn Mountains that formed a dark purple, jagged-peaked background, but along the ridge McGlory could see red-blanketed Indians riding back and forth on their horses, and flashing mirrors were signalling up there.

'Do you see that, McGlory?' Carrington spat out his words. 'That is Lodge Trail Ridge, and from up there Red Cloud watches our every move. There is nothing for you out there, McGlory, but death and destruction. Build yourself a temporary corral outside of the walls, McGlory, and await my instructions. Captain Flynn, escort our guests to the gate.'

Abruptly dismissed by the colonel,

the McGlorys walked with Captain Flynn. They passed the parade ground where the now stationary military band played the last few bars of 'Hail Columbia'. The Reverend Lionel Anthom strode across the parade ground and mounted a small rostrum as the last notes of the band became echoes before fading.

'Let us pray, my brothers and sisters,' Anthom cried out to the small crowd that had been listening to the band. 'We are the children . . . '

The preacher broke off, mouth dropping open in surprise as he saw the McGlorys walking by. They both waved a hand to him, but kept going with Flynn so that Anthom couldn't catch up with them. Within minutes they could hear his booming voice resume his preaching. They were too far away to detect whether or not he was speaking in rhyme.

They passed a large tent, the flaps of which were open and a smell of alcohol came out through to them. Pulling a face, Flynn explained, 'That's Harry Hill's place; the last days of Babylon. It's a den of vice, intoxication and fornication. There's only one rule in there, and it's painted on a sign that's hanging up. Do you know what that sign says? It reads 'Gentlemen will not smoke when dancing with ladies'. It's ludicrous. We humans are a funny lot. Whether we are saints or sinners, we behave strangely when death can be seen approaching.'

'And you believe that death is approaching Fort Kearney?' Kitty asked.

They passed a platoon of soldiers struggling with howitzers, the man-handling of the heavy guns bringing sweat to their brows. All came to attention and the senior soldier threw up a salute that Captain Flynn returned.

'I am in no doubt of it,' Flynn replied to Kitty's query. 'Once Red Cloud has the tribes organized, then he'll hit us. This fort is a mistake. We are surrounded by hills that shut off all observation of the surrounding terrain, we have no cover between the fort and the water supply, while the nearest supply of timber and fuel is five miles away. When the snow falls Red Cloud need only surround the fort, cut off our communications so that we either starve or surrender. What do you intend to do, McGlory?'

'I don't reckon as how I can afford to tangle with the army, Captain,' McGlory answered, 'so I guess I'll build myself a corral like the colonel said.'

McGlory started on this immediately after Flynn had left him and Kitty at the gate. He worked his men hard, including Sieber, and within three hours a sturdy but temporary corral had been erected close to the wall of the fort. It was about the time that rawhide was being tied tight around the final post that Captain Flynn rode out, his military manner correct because a young subaltern rode at his side.

'Compliments of Colonel Carrington, Mr McGlory,' the captain began. 'He has issued an order that you dismantle this corral and rebuild it three miles out.'

'Three miles!' McGlory exclaimed, an angry Kitty at his side and his men grumbling a little way off. 'Three miles out, Captain, and we won't get any protection from the fort. You wouldn't get to us in time if we were hit.'

Face impassive, Captain Flynn kept his eyes on a distant horizon. 'Those are the Colonel's orders, Mr McGlory. We are expecting a company of cavalry at any time, and the grass in close to the walls is required for their mounts. The Colonel's orders are that you must construct your corral three miles from the fort, and remain there until he considers it safe to give you permission to leave.'

Giving a salute, Flynn wheeled his horse about, the subaltern making the same move, as close as a shadow. After riding only a yard or so, the captain reined up, dismounted and made a pretence of tightening the cinch of his saddle. McGlory walked up to him. The subaltern waited just feet away.

Making his words part of his breathing so that McGlory had to lean close to hear them, Flynn said. 'Hit the trail tonight, Joe. Get out of it, otherwise you, Kitty and the others will be dead by dawn.'

Mounting up once more, Captain Flynn rode away without a backward glance, and McGlory walked back to his complaining men to make them moan even more by ordering that the corral they had just spent so much energy building be dismantled.

It was late afternoon when they had put a distance of around three miles between the herd and the fort. Grady rode up to ask McGlory, 'Do I start the men building another corral, Joe?'

'No,' McGlory shook his head. 'Let the men have their chow, Matt, then I want them all gathered here, even those riding herd. I won't keep them long.'

The sun was more than half below the horizon when the cowboys grouped

161

together in a half-circle for McGlory to address them. Kitty stood a little way off, close enough to hear what was being said, but far enough away not to encroach upon the man's world that her husband regarded as sacrosanct. Judy wasn't present. Apart from looking after Sieber, and enjoying a deepening friendship with Kitty, the mystery woman stayed aloof from the general life of the trail herd. Sieber, too, remained detached to a large extent, but he was a hard worker and stood in the line-up of men now.

'I'll give it to you straight,' McGlory began. 'I have been ordered by Colonel Carrington not to move on north. But out here we are just as exposed to an attack by hostiles as we would be back on the trail.'

'I reckons as how youse going to ask us whether we want to be killed here or somewheres along the Bozeman, boss,' Clancy Magee said, cleaning a pan he had brought with him.

'I don't view it quite like that,'

162

McGlory disagreed, 'but I am saying that I intend to move the herd on tonight. I'm giving you all the choice of coming along or staying here at the fort. No one is going to make you go or stay. It's up to you, and now is the time to make up your mind. If you want to stay, there'll be no hard feelings.'

No one stepped out of the line or spoke up, and McGlory used a nod to thank the men, before asking, 'What say you, Sieber, you staying or going?'

'I'm sticking with you,' Sieber replied in his rasping way, ensuring that the double meaning in his words was explicit.

'And that woman of yours?' McGlory enquired.

'I, too, will go with you!'

Judy's voice answered clearly on her own behalf, although she remained unseen. The shadows were lengthening fast and McGlory spoke urgently. 'I want to move out in half an hour. We won't get far tonight, as the beef can't be pushed until they get back into the notion of moving. You've had your chuck time, so Clancy doesn't have any more cooking to do. Are you ready to move out, Magee?'

'I ain't never bin known to hold up no drive,' Clancy Magee answered tetchily.

The men were moving away, but Limm Sieber walked casually up to McGlory to say, 'There's a rider coming up on us, kind of slow like.'

'I know,' McGlory said, aware of the significance of just Sieber and himself having heard the barely audible sound in the night.

'We share instincts and reflexes that make us dangerous for each other, Apache Joe,' Sieber said softly, not once having used McGlory's real name in front of anyone since joining the herd. 'You want me to make a move before he gets here?'

'No,' McGlory replied, walking to pick up his rifle where he had left it resting against Kitty's buggy. 'Let him come.'

When the rider, his huge bulk exaggerated by the dusk he came slowly out of, was within earshot, McGlory's cold voice said, 'Hold it right there, stranger.'

'Is that you, Apache Joe?' the rider enquired in a hoarse whisper.

'It's Joe McGlory,' McGlory said, lowering his rifle and stepping forward. 'What are you looking for, Preacher?'

The Reverend Lionel Anthom, the rider, dismounted clumsily and with a number of complaining grunts, spoke to McGlory as he unsteadily reached the ground. 'As a Christian, Apa ... McGlory, I am invoking the tenet of one good turn deserving another. I am requesting that you permit me and my wagon to accompany you to Virginia City.'

'I guess I owe you more than that, Preacher,' McGlory said, 'but even if I agree, Colonel Carrington's permission is needed for a gate to be opened, and he's not going to let you bring your wagon out.'

'I have come to an arrangement with a senior officer,' Anthom assured McGlory.

Captain Flynn, McGlory concluded. The camp adjutant was busily engaged in helping people against all his military training and inclinations. That said something about the dangers Fort Phil Kearney was facing.

'Then you'd better get moving, Preacher, because we're hitting the trail very shortly,' McGlory said, adding a question, 'Are you travelling alone?'

There was the hint of a chuckle in Anthom's voice as he answered, 'I have but one poor companion with me on the road to Damascus. You did meet him on one occasion: his name is William.'

7

Dawn was less than an hour away and the wolf cries had been going on out in the night for some time. McGlory was perturbed by the fact that they lacked a certain authenticity. He had ridden right round the herd to warn the drovers to be additionally alert, and to check that they all had their Remington rifles loaded and at the ready. Now, back riding beside the buggy occupied by Kitty and Judy, he was becoming more uneasy as the sound of wolves moved closer. Coming up close behind the buggy was the Reverend Anthom's wagon, with the preacher holding the reins and William the executioner on the seat beside him.

'What ails thee, brother?' the preacher called as McGlory let his horse slow so that he was being overtaken.

'Just going to take a look around,'

McGlory called back.

Then a rider came out of the night to fall in beside him. It was Limm Sieber, his eyes, peering over a bandanna pulled up over his mouth and nose as a protection against dust when riding drag, his voice muffled by it when he spoke to McGlory.

'I've never heard a wolf sound like that,' Sieber said.

'Wolves or not, they're getting too close,' McGlory said, letting his horse drop further back and reining to the right, ready to ride away from the herd.

'You need at least one man siding you out there,' Sieber warned.

'If I did I'd take Matt Grady.'

Sieber snorted. 'He's a cattleman not a gunman, McGlory. You'd only get him killed.'

'But he's not likely to put a bullet in my back,' McGlory retorted.

Riding in close to him, Sieber pulled down the bandanna. The stubbly beard made his face even harder, and his eyes were glinting angrily as he glared at McGlory. The cry of a wolf came from close by, and Sieber waited for it to be answered before he spoke. When the second cry came he gave a nod of satisfaction then spoke in his gruff way.

'I'll repeat the promise I made to you and myself, Apache Joe. I'm going to get you, but when I do it won't be from behind.'

'I guess I can take your word for that,' McGlory acknowledged. 'Come on.'

They rode off a short way from the herd before both of them, in an instinctive, unspoken agreement, dismounted and ground-hitched their horses.

Hurrying through the night, side-by-side, bent double, moving silently, they dropped into a hollow and lay on their backs, brushwood all around them, listening.

The cry of a wolf came from their left, and McGlory pointed to his own chest. When the expected answering cry came, McGlory pointed at Sieber, who nodded and slid away on his belly to the right, the direction from which the second cry had come.

As he crawled along, McGlory regretted bringing his rifle with him. Sieber had left his with his horse. Doing that was risky if an Indian should get to the horses before they returned, but McGlory was finding the weapon to be an encumbrance. He lay it across his shoulders as he crawled, holding the rifle with one hand. It made his movements awkward, but it avoided the disaster of having the firearm knock against a stone.

Waiting for the wolf cry to come again, McGlory paused in a silence disturbed only by the whispering of some tall grass moved by a gentle pre-dawn breeze. There was no other movement, which was a tribute to Sieber's skills. It would have been easy for McGlory to believe that the bounty hunter wasn't out there in the darkness.

From just ahead of him the cry went up, clever enough to perhaps fool a wolf. There was an immediate answer from McGlory's right, which told him that Sieber had not yet got his man. The calls had become more frequent, suggesting that the Indians were moving into position for an attack. He crawled round a rock that was no more than one foot high. From the sound he had just heard he expected to see a redskin squatting, preparing to signal once more.

But an astounded McGlory saw only empty space in front of him. Too late, he realized that he had been duped. McGlory was turning, not sure what to expect, not yet in a position to defend himself, when a dark figure sprang off the rock to land heavily on his back. Although winded, McGlory rolled, taking the man on his back with him, and they parted, both springing to their feet.

McGlory's rifle had been knocked from his grasp, and he wasted a split second deciding whether to go for his six-gun or his knife. The delay was a costly one for McGlory. Facing him, wearing a warbonnet, was a Cheyenne warrior, young and powerful. The Indian was holding a rifle in both hands, and he used it to good effect. Swinging it low he caught McGlory a cracking blow on the knees with the stock. Sickened by the pain, McGlory was collapsing. Although he could see the Cheyenne bringing the rifle up, there was nothing McGlory could do to avoid the knock-out blow as the butt cracked against the side of his head.

When he came round it was in the half light of dawn. Lying on damp-smelling grass, a dull ache in his head that became worse as he opened his eyes. The side of his face, from the left cheekbone upwards, was sore. Blinking a couple of times to clear a mist from his eyes, McGlory saw the Cheyenne who had felled him. The Indian was sitting with his back against a tree, and the first odd thing that McGlory noticed was that the Cheyenne no longer had his rifle. Then, as his senses fully returned, McGlory knew from the Indian's glazed eyes and drooping-open mouth that he was dead.

Sensing someone behind him, McGlory groggily raised himself up onto one elbow and turned his head slowly. Sitting on the rock from which the Cheyenne had launched himself at McGlory, was a half-breed with a tentative smile on his dark face. An astonished McGlory had to look twice before he could convince himself that he wasn't mistaken.

'Luis!' he exclaimed.

'You took a lot of finding, Apache Joe, but I'm back with you,' the part-Indian said.

Delighted to have a trusted member of his old renegade band with him, McGlory looked from the dead Cheyenne to Luis, a question evident in his facial expression.

'Just happened along at the right time,' Luis said with a nod to confirm that he had killed the Indian. 'He was just about to stove in the back of your skull with the stock of his rifle.'

Raising up his rear end, McGlory knelt with his head low to let blood flow back into it. He heard Luis tell him, 'Sieber's gone to get your horses. He got the other Cheyenne, Joe. They were scouts, so as they won't be reporting back I guess your herd is safe, at least for a time.'

Getting up on to his feet, standing for a moment to let his spinning brain settle, McGlory saw that Luis had a pinto pony hitched to some brushwood. The easy way that the 'breed had mentioned Sieber's name prompted a question from McGlory.

'Do you know Sieber, Luis?'

'We was in a tough spot together once,' Luis nodded. 'He can handle himself. He's a good man, Joe.'

'He's a bounty hunter, and he's sworn to get me when we reach Montana,' McGlory said bitterly.

'I guess that's between you and

Sieber,' the half-breed shrugged. 'My money's on you, Joe, but he'll take some beating. Anyways, I'd like to go to Montana with you if you'll have me.'

'I wouldn't ask for anyone better to side me, Luis,' McGlory assured him. 'Just remember that I'm not Apache Joe now.'

Luis gave him a white-toothed grin. 'I've been on your trail long enough to learn that, Joe McGlory.'

Sieber came back then, riding his horse and leading McGlory's. When all three of them were mounted and had set off for where the herd would be waiting, McGlory began asking himself questions. He had failed badly when going after the Cheyenne scout, and he would be dead had it not been for Luis. Since his savage fight with Grey Eagle he had been disciplining himself so as to become more civilized to fit in with his new life. Now it seemed that this self-control had seriously affected his abilities as a fighting man. It looked as if he either had to revert to being his old wild self, or risk never getting to Montana. The half-breed, who always had the knack of knowing what was going on inside the heads of other people, broke into his thoughts.

'Take care, Joe,' Luis said, 'that in learning the ways of a cattleman you don't forget the ways of the Apache.'

Knowing to what the half-breed was referring, McGlory admitted, 'I wasn't what I should be back there.'

'I've never seen you like that. It was nothing like the Apache Joe I used to know,' Luis said, then he turned to Sieber who had been riding a little apart from the other two. 'You need to keep a watch over your shoulder, Sieber. There's a Sioux tracking you down.'

'Does he wear an army uniform?' Sieber enquired.

'That's him,' the half-breed confirmed.

'You missed one hostile when you hit that encampment, McGlory,' Sieber said, not critically but as a comment.

'I'm not rightly sure who that Sioux wants most, Sieber, you or that woman you've got with you,' the half-breed remarked. 'Though I reckon that he doesn't want her dead like he does you.'

Sieber didn't comment on this, but he quickened the pace of his horse a little, anxious to get back to the herd to protect Judy. But as they topped a ridge the sound of shots came up to them. It was no concern of theirs, for the herd was still a few miles away up ahead, but they reined up and sat on their horses looking down into a shallow canyon.

A life and death battle was going on in pine woods down below them. Soldiers on a wood-cutting detail were pinned down by a small force of shouting Sioux that was circling them. One soldier was signalling back to the fort frantically, but even if the request was answered, help couldn't reach them in time to save them.

As the three men watched, the Sioux moved in. While some stayed on their horses to continue circling, others dismounted and moved in on the soldiers. There was a terrible screaming then. It didn't seem possible that it came from a man. It was unearthly, horrible to hear, and McGlory knew what it was before he heard Luis murmur, 'They're scalping some poor cuss alive down there.'

'Spread out as we go down,' McGlory ordered, not doubting for a moment that the other two would follow as he went down the slope at a gallop.

Seeing them coming, the Sioux who had dismounted climbed back onto their horses. The whole band kept circling the soldiers they had pinned down, and were ready to meet the assault from McGlory and his two companions.

They rode straight at the Sioux. Ahead of the others, McGlory wheeled his horse to the right, going over the side of it in the Apache way, keeping the body of the horse between the Sioux and himself. Riding through a hail of lead and a bombardment of swishing arrows, McGlory turned at the end of the line of Sioux, coming up over the horse's back to cut three Indians down with rifle fire.

Only two soldiers were left standing, and they were in no condition to assist McGlory, Sieber, and Luis, who were outnumbered something like five to one.

Two Sioux braves rode close to the wood cart, jumping from their horses onto it, standing on it with rifles to their shoulders, planning to have the cart as a barrier that they and the other braves could shelter behind while fighting. They fired bullet after bullet but miraculously missed Luis, who was riding straight at the cart on which they were standing. As he got closer, oblivious to the lead singing all around him, Luis, a magnificent horseman, stood upright, perfectly balanced, on the back of his horse. Although it didn't slow, the horse veered to its left just before it seemed it must smash into the cart. The half-breed leapt as the horse turned. Holding his rifle horizontally at around eye-level, he landed on the cart between the two Sioux, each end of his rifle connecting with their faces slammingly, the impetus snapping their necks as it knocked them backwards off the cart.

Luis was behind the cart then, firing at the other Indians who still circled on their horses. Sieber came riding in between them, firing as he came, causing them to lose concentration as they avoided him. Reaching the cart he stepped off his horse on to it, then jumped down to the ground beside the half-breed.

Cut off from the cart by the mounted Sioux, McGlory rode this way and that, firing his rifle, dodging bullets. Then he reined up his horse and let out a war cry. With superb skill he rode at the nearest Sioux, leaping out of the saddle, taking the Indian off the back of his horse so that they hit the ground together. Getting swiftly to his feet, McGlory grabbed at the Sioux with his left hand, bringing the Indian up off the ground and stabbing him to death in one rapid movement.

Sheathing his bloodied knife as three Sioux rode down on him, McGlory used superhuman strength to lift the dead Indian above his head. Elbows locked, McGlory threw the corpse at the advancing Indian riders. The body coming through the air, and the rank stench of blood, caused the Sioux ponies to rear up on to their hind legs, screeching. Two of the Sioux were unseated. In a fraction of a second, McGlory was on them, slashing the throat of one, kicking the other hard enough in the head to snap his neck.

The third Sioux calmed his mount and came riding at McGlory, who turned to look for his horse. With the animal too far away to be reached, he could do nothing but stand and face the oncoming Sioux, who was intent on riding McGlory into the ground. A shot from either Luis or Sieber knocked the Indian off the horse. Doing a smart side-step, McGlory wrapped his arms round the neck of the animal as it went charging past him. Carried along by the momentum of the horse, McGlory took steps that were long and became increasingly bounding until after one hugely loping stretch of his legs he bounced himself up on to the back of the Sioux horse.

Chased by mounted Indians, two of whom were brought down by rifle fire from Sieber and the half-breed, McGlory released some lusty Apache yells as he headed for the cart. As he leapt over the top of the cart, clearing the heads of Luis and Sieber, forced to somersault, rolling on his shoulders to come up smoothly on to his feet, McGlory heard a bugle blast somewhere in the middle distance.

The Sioux also heard it, and they broke away, leaving McGlory and his two companions amid the wounded, the dying and the dead soldiers who had made up the woodcutting party. Their comrades would soon be there to care for them, and McGlory was aware that, having left the fort without the permission of Colonel Carrington, he was in no position to be around when the approaching soldiers arrived.

'Let's move out,' he said as the Sioux disappeared over the ridge.

They hurried from the cart to round up their horses, ignoring the groaning of the injured soldiers lying around them. But then McGlory paused as from the corner of his eye he saw a captain's insignia on a shoulder above a blood-soaked chest. He checked again, and although Sieber urged him to keep moving, McGlory knelt beside the injured officer.

It was Captain Flynn, his face ashen, drained of blood by the terrible wound in his chest. Trying to say something, he coughed blood. McGlory had begun to carefully unbutton Flynn's tunic when the officer found his voice, even though it was weak and rattling from

183

blood in his throat.

'There's nothing you can do for me except say goodbye, McGlory,' Flynn said.

Nodding agreement because grown men shouldn't attempt to fool each other, McGlory let go of the jacket and asked the captain, 'Is there anything I can do for you?'

'Not for me,' Flynn smiled weakly but courageously. 'But if you reach Montana, and come back down the Bozeman Trail, then please tell my wife that I died instantly and without pain. I don't want her to know that I went slow and hard.'

'I'll tell her,' McGlory promised, but his words were wasted on a dead man.

Mounting up and riding after Luis and Sieber, who had gone only at a trot so that he could catch up, McGlory admired Flynn for his total disregard of self while his final thoughts had been of the woman he loved. Sentiment was something he had learned nothing of in his upbringing, and he wasn't at ease with it.

They rode in silence until they came to the herd, which Grady had decided to rest for the day. He suggested to McGlory, 'It's up to you, boss, but the way I see it, moving the herd at night and resting up in the day could be the best way.'

'We'll give it a try,' McGlory agreed. 'Whichever way we do it I want to be at the Yellowstone before the snow flies.'

'I reckon that could depend on the Sioux and the other Indians, Joe,' Luis gave his opinion. 'On my way up I saw plenty of activity. The tribes are gathering together.'

The subject of likely troubles ahead came up again when McGlory was sitting beside Kitty eating with the guests she had invited to their fire. Luis, a loner, didn't wait around to be asked. He was off eating on his own somewhere. The two races in Luis were not balanced. He was more savage than a civilized man.

Judy, as silent as ever, pride in the way she sat and moved, was beside Kitty, and Sieber sat at the other side of her. Across the fire from McGlory was the Reverend Lionel Anthom and William the Hangman, their features dramatized by the dancing flames of the fire.

'I shall hold a short prayer meeting before we move out, McGlory,' Anthom said, his voice as booming in conversation as when preaching. 'We will need the help of the Lord to reach Montana now that the tribes are gathering.'

'We've no time for praying, Preacher,' McGlory said bluntly. 'You put your faith where you like, Anthom. I've placed mine in our Remington rifles.'

William quoted the Bible at McGlory: "I do not look to men for honour. But with you it is different, as I know well, for you have no love of God in you'.'

'John, chapter five, verses 41 and 42,' Anthom said in qualification.

'Keep it shut, William,' McGlory harshly advised. 'I'm not real easy about taking a hangman along with us.'

Anthom said, 'You are a man of fickle opinions, McGlory. You overlook the fact that William did not hang you, while you break bread with a man who will kill you once we reach Montana. Dead or alive, McGlory, Sieber will be paid once the law in Virginia City is informed that you are the infamous Apache Joe.'

At this, Sieber rose and walked slowly off into the darkness. Looking at his retreating figure for a moment, Judy then stood and followed him. Not all the food had been eaten nor the coffee drunk, but the meal was over. The Reverend Anthom and William walked away as Kitty and McGlory threw the remainder of the coffee from their mugs on to the fire. Through the hissing steam that resulted, McGlory saw the man he had appointed as his foreman walking by.

'Get ready to move out, Grady,' he called.

'You got it, boss,' Grady shouted back.

As she walked with McGlory towards her buggy, where Judy was standing waiting for her, Kitty slowed her pace to quietly ask, 'What are you going to do about Sieber, Joe?'

'What would you have me do, Kit?' McGlory replied, a little absently because his eyes were seeking the North Star, his mind already on the trail.

'Luis would tend to him for you before we get to Montana.'

Swinging his head sharply to look at her, McGlory's voice hissed as he told her, 'That's the past, Kitty. I want no more of that.'

'Our pasts are dogging us,' she pointed out miserably.

'Then we have to get away from them,' McGlory said, his eyes lighting up with ambition. 'We're going to make this drive, Kit. I'm going to be the man who starts up Montana ranching with Texas cattle. We'll get this herd there and settled, then we'll move back down the Bozeman Trail to organize another drive.'

McGlory leaned his back against a sapling that the elements had made as tough and durable as he was. Relaxing, his hard face was peaceful as he allowed his dream to run leisurely through his head. Unable to share his confidence in the future, Kitty rested an anxious hand on his arm.

'Are you sure you're doing right to force yourself to change, Joe?' she asked.

'I'm not changing, Kit, I'm set to become the real me,' he answered. 'For many years I wrongly believed myself to be an Apache, but now I know that I am a white man, and I will behave like a white man.'

'There are many wicked white men, Joe,' Kitty cautioned him.

He nodded. 'I know that. But I was a good Apache once, so I will be a good white man.'

With the conversation over as far as he was concerned, McGlory was walking away to his horse when Kitty called to him, 'What of the Sieber business?'

'Tonight I move the herd along the trail,' he replied, without halting or even turning his head. 'Tomorrow, or some day after tomorrow, is when Sieber will have to be faced.'

When Kitty reached where Judy waited, the other woman asked, 'Did I hear Limm's name mentioned, Kitty?'

'Yes.'

'How will this end, Kitty?' an unhappy Judy enquired.

Busy harnessing a horse to the buggy, Kitty asked a question of her own without looking up. 'How do you want it, Judy, wrapped up in vain hopes or straight from the hip?'

'Hit me with it straight, Kitty,' Judy replied, the confidence in her voice totally absent from the expression of anxiety on her pretty face.

'One or both of them will end up dead,' Kitty said flatly.

'Why?' Judy exclaimed despairingly.

'Since Limm joined up with this trail drive he's gained a lot of respect for Joe.'

'But that won't stop him trying to kill him,' a cynical Kitty answered.

'Only because of one reason, Kitty.'

'What's that?'

'Because Limm knows that McGlory killed a man to escape execution,' Judy explained. 'He says he can't forgive a man for doing something like that to save his own skin.'

'Sieber would soon forgive Joe if he knew who that man was, Judy.'

Hope lightening her face, Judy double-checked. 'Is that the truth, Kitty?'

'God's gospel truth,' Kitty said as she mounted up in the buggy.

Climbing up beside her, Judy requested, 'I'll tell Limm right away. Who was the man, Kitty?'

'I can't tell you, Judy, it's Joe's business.'

'Then I'll ask Joe,' a determined Judy declared.

'Don't waste your time, woman,' Kitty told her. 'He won't tell you.'

'But don't you care if they kill each other, Kitty?'

Annoyed by the question, Kitty snapped, 'Of course I care. But it's like caring whether or not this herd stampedes before sun-up. There's just nothing you nor I can do about it, Judy.'

8

They had been making good progress by travelling at night. McGlory estimated that they covered fifteen miles every twenty-four hours. Although they'd had Indian problems, they had been no more than skirmishes in which the redskins had retreated when faced with the rapid-fire rifles of the cowboys. It was after they had forked east from the Bozeman Trail that heavy rain started problems for them.

'It could have been worse,' Luis said, the collar of his slicker high, eyes screwed up against the driving rain. 'Just a bit colder and this would be a blizzard.'

But that optimistic outlook on the part of the half-breed faded when they reached Clark's Fork and they saw how swollen it was. Sitting on their horses side by side, McGlory, Sieber and Luis looked at the rapidly swirling waters, the hissing roar of the river hammering at their eardrums. What they saw here didn't bode well for when they would reach the Yellowstone.

'It'll be a mighty tough crossing, McGlory,' Sieber predicted, the odd relationship between Apache Joe and himself set aside for the remainder of the drive.

Yet when they got to the Yellowstone River, that prophesy proved inadequate. On a gloomy dark day, with the rain coming down in torrents, crossing the river seemed impossible. A wind had risen that not only drove the rain into them harder, but whipped up waves on the river so that it was difficult to gauge its depth and the suitability of the banks each side for making a crossing.

The only good factor was that the heavy rain kept the cattle subdued, thereby lessening the chances of a stampede. But as they held the cattle in tight while McGlory planned the crossing, a rider named Baines, a gnarled veteran of trail drives, rode his horse into a ditch. Unseated, Baines was lying in thick mud, the restless edge of the river lapping over his legs, when Luis shouted an order at him.

'Lift your hands over your head,' Luis called, his voice battling against the storm.

When Baines obeyed, Luis lassoed him at the first attempt. The rope around his chest, Baines lowered his arms so that Luis could use his horse to pull the fallen rider away from the river.

'Could be badly sprained, most likely broke,' Clancy Magee diagnosed as he looked at Baines's damaged right leg.

'Put him up on the chuck wagon,' McGlory instructed, adding, 'I want everything across before the light fades today.'

They got to work then, not noticing the driving rain as they laboured. A raft was built and all of the provisions and blankets were loaded on to it.

'You two get up in the chuckwagon,'

McGlory shouted at Kitty and Judy, who had been huddling together in the meagre shelter under the wagon. 'We'll float you across in it. But first the beef has to go. You tend to Baines.'

They both nodded, aware that the storm would defeat female voices. With the two women safely in the wagon, McGlory walked away until he became aware that Magee was following him.

'Where you heading, Magee?' McGlory yelled above a wind that was increasing.

'Help you get the cattle across,' the cook shouted back.

Lifting both arms to wave them in a crossing fashion to dismiss Magee's notion, McGlory shouted, 'We've got punchers to do that. Nobody else but you can get that chuckwagon across the Yellowstone, Clancy. Stay with it. Your chance will come.'

Leaving the cook, McGlory mounted up, riding his horse, slithering and sliding, down to the bank of the river. He gave the signal and the crossing of the cattle began.

It was a hazardous task that went on throughout the day. McGlory knew that he was building up a problem for himself by leaving the cattle unsupervized once they were on the far side of the river. But he couldn't spare men to keep them in check. He didn't have as many riders as he would have liked to get them across.

In mid-afternoon, when close to half the herd had been shifted, tragedy struck. A wave that had been built up somewhere far up the river, slappingly hit the east bank of the crossing cows. Several panicked, and as they threshed about, a crazed steer, its eyes wide and bright, leapt up to scramble over the backs of them. The steer made it, but tumbled off the back of the last cow, colliding with a young cowboy, knocking his horse sideways and unsaddling him.

Tossed into the wild waters, the cowboy went down. Watching it happen from a short distance away, McGlory could tell that the current would take the cowboy under the cattle.

'It's Tex!' a rider cried, urging his horse through the water to where he had seen his buddy disappear.

'Get back to your position,' Luis shouted at the cowboy, but others were coming to assist him.

Left to themselves the cattle were slowing in mid-stream, the edges of the herd fraying, spreading out. McGlory joined Luis in shouting at the men to get back to where they had been. But they either weren't heard or were ignored.

It was Limm Sieber who pushed his horse through the turbulent water to reach the first rider who had broken away in the hope of rescuing his pal. Taking his lariat from his saddle, keeping it coiled, Sieber swung it. The rope caught the rider cruelly across the face. Blood flowed to immediately become diluted by the rain. Reining up, the rider looked undecided for a moment. In pain, he would have doubtless tried to draw on Sieber had he not been wearing a slicker as protection against the rain.

Coming to his senses, the rider, wiping a copious flow of blood from his face, moved back into position, as did the other cowboys. Soon the herd was back under control, bunched as tightly as possible on its way to the far bank.

Swimming his horse close to Sieber, McGlory raised a hand in appreciation of what the bounty hunter had done. Sieber made no sign of recognition of the gesture of thanks. They both looked to the far side of the herd then. 'Tex' had surfaced there. His clothing and skin ripped to shreds by the slashing of hundreds of sharp hoofs, the drowned cowboy drifted off down the river. The sight was made all the more sorrowful by the animation given the body by the rough surface of the water. It gave the appearance of life when there was only death.

'Here's the last coming up,' Luis shouted, and McGlory turned to see that the final cow was in the water.

This gave the weary cowboys enough heart to finish the crossing with a final surge. Dismounting on the far bank, each one of the riders dropped in exhaustion as soon as they hit the ground. They lay in the mud, too tired to take any notice of the rain lashing down on them.

Although every bit as tired as the hands, McGlory, Sieber and Luis swam their horses back across the river. Using ropes, they pulled the fully loaded raft down to the edge of the water so that the angry waves smashed themselves against it. As if it had been agreed among the three of them, Luis pulled off his waterproof clothing. Then the half-breed stripped until he was naked to the waist, his dark skin shining with rain, the sheen enhancing the sleek look of his well-muscled body. Tying the end of a rope around his middle, the other end being fastened to the raft, Luis walked into the water and then started to swim.

With strong, lengthy strokes, the half-Indian battled against the waves and the current. After what seemed ages to the watching and waiting McGlory and Sieber, Luis reached the other side. Crawling out on to a bank that had been smashed into rough, slippery mud by the herd, he knelt on all fours, resting for a moment. Then he was up on his feet, untying the rope and waving an arm to McGlory.

McGlory and Sieber pushed the raft the final few feet into the water. Mounting up, they rode their horses into the water and swam them across. It would have been easier but riskier to take the rope across in this manner. A horse, particularly a tired one, is skittish and liable to panic if hit by a floating log or something similar. If that had happened the rope from the raft would have been difficult to recover.

They reached the other side, dismounting to join Luis on the rope, tugging on it.

'Come on, you men!' McGlory shouted.

Most of the men lay still, but about six got up and staggered through the mud to take hold of the rope. Tired out, soaked to the skin, they pulled and got the raft over in tight to the bank. More of the men stood then, bodies sagging in weariness as they slithered through the mud to take their place on the rope. Digging feet in hard to get a foothold, the men finally got the raft far enough up the bank to be safe from the river.

Making sure the raft was secured, McGlory mounted up again. As he wheeled his horse towards the river, he saw only a few cows standing around, shivering. A round-up was going to be necessary. It would be a long job because his men would first need a night's sleep. He rode down to the river, Sieber riding behind him, while Luis climbed bareback on to a stray horse from the remuda, and followed them.

Back on the other bank, Luis, still bare to the waist but unmindful of the cold, wind, and rain, tied the rope fixed to the front of the chuckwagon around his waist. As he walked down to the water, Kitty and Judy put their heads out through the canvas.

'Is it all right, Joe?' Kitty asked anxiously.

'We've got the herd across, Kit, but the beef are scattered.'

'We'll get them back together,' Kitty said confidently.

'You girls get back in there and hang on tight,' Sieber advised. 'This is going to be one rough ride.'

The Reverend Lionel Anthom and William were standing forlornly beside their little wagon, trying unsuccessfully to shelter from the torrential rain and howling wind. The least of McGlory's worries, they would cross last.

'Let her rip, Joe,' Magee shouted as they rolled the wagon down to the bank.

Luis had swum to the other side, and

now he and at least ten of the cowboys were hauling on the rope. Getting on to their horses, McGlory and Sieber swam the animals one on each side of the wagon as it went into the water, steadying it.

The chuckwagon, laden with pots and victuals, floated heavy in the water, fighting the powerful waves rather than riding them. Reaching the centre of the river it rocked dangerously as it became exposed fully to the wind. McGlory and Sieber clung on at each side, doing their best to use their bodies as ballast to keep the wagon upright. They succeeded and, drained of energy though they were, the cowboys pulling on the rope let out a ragged cheer as the front wheels of the chuckwagon touched lightly against the bank.

From his vantage point high up on the wagon, Clancy Magee was the first one to see the huge wave rolling down river towards them, and he cried out, his shriek rising above the wind and rain. 'Lookee out!'

McGlory heard the shouted warning just as the wave hit him. Swept out of the saddle, he fought to keep his head above water as his clothing dragged him down. Watching helplessly, he saw the wagon tilt precariously away from him. Pots and pans came rattling out to splash into the water and float away. Bags of beans and coffee tumbled into the water to sink as the wagon teetered. He saw the men, led by Luis, running into the river to grab at the wagon, trying to stop it from going on its side. He shouted pointlessly, because he couldn't be heard, as he saw Kitty and Judy reaching out, trying to stop any more utensils or provisions from falling into the water.

Then a second wave hit and the wagon went on to its side, pitching Clancy Magee head first into the bank. McGlory saw Sieber's horse, its neck broken, float away from the other side of the wagon. He had to assume that Sieber had been crushed, and found himself regretting the death of the bounty hunter, when he saw Judy thrown out of the back of the chuckwagon into the churning water of the river.

Tugging out of his outer clothing, McGlory pulled it off, going under water, filling his lungs with it as he did so. Coming up, coughing, spewing out the muddy, foul-smelling water, he saw that the men had succeeded in getting the wagon upright. They were pulling it up on to the bank, driven by the shouted curses of Clancy Magee. Luis was going into the water, but McGlory knew that the half-breed was unaware that Judy had gone overboard. Luis was searching for Sieber.

Free of his heavy clothing now, his lungs as clear of water as he could hope to get them, McGlory struck out downstream. He couldn't see anything of Judy but that was the direction in which the current would be taking her.

Trying to stay in the centre of the river, judging that to be the best viewing point to catch sight of Judy, McGlory had to swim twice as hard to stay there. Abandoning that idea, letting himself be swept in closer to the bank, he kept his head as high as possible in an attempt at seeing over the waves.

Something caught his eye some thirty yards ahead. Needing to wait for three particularly high waves to pass, McGlory could then catch a glimpse of the colour of the dress Judy had been wearing. Was it just the dress, having been ripped off in the strong current, or was Judy still in it? He struck out strongly, pulling himself through the water at speed so that he soon could see that Judy was still wearing the dress. She was caught up in a tangle of long branches, most of her body under the surface, her hair flowing out in the water.

Swimming in close he could see that she was on her back. Water was lapping over Judy's face. Her mouth was open, her eyes closed. In these conditions, McGlory told himself, there was little chance of her being alive.

Moving into the shallows he managed to get a footing in the mud. Standing, the water up to his chest, McGlory untangled the branches from the woman's dress. Her body was cold, but not stiff. He told himself that immersion in the water was responsible for the coldness, and the fact that her body was flexible heartened him.

Crooking his arm under Judy's head, he held it so that the water no longer washed into her mouth. Then put his other arm under her knees. Back against the river bank, he climbed up slowly, bending a knee at a time, digging in a heel to get a purchase. It took a long time, and every one of his muscles was heavily taxed, but at last he got the woman up on level ground. Even so, with the rain still tipping down they were both as wet as when they had been in the river. With a thumb he gently lifted one of Judy's eyelids. Only the white showed, and this worried him.

Giving himself no more than a brief moment to recover, McGlory rolled Judy over on to her stomach. Making sure that her head was turned to one side, he straddled her at the waist, without allowing any of his weight to rest on her. Then, with both hands flat on her back over the lungs, he gave on and off pressure. Trying to keep to a fine line between being hard enough to force water out of her lungs, but not so hard that he cracked her ribs, McGlory kept going for some time without results.

Disappointed, he eased off, sitting upright to get his breath. Ready to give up and carry the body back to the others, he rocked to one side to get off the woman. One knee slipped in the mud, and the other hit Judy hard in the back before McGlory could get his hands down into the mud to steady himself. Contrite, he was reminding himself that he couldn't harm a corpse, when Judy made a harsh rattling noise in her throat.

Doubting that he had heard the noise, McGlory was then snapped into action as some kind of eruption went on inside Judy. Then water came gushingly out of her mouth. More of a slurry of mud than water, it gurgled out continuously as body-racking coughs hit the woman, convulsing her body. Getting back into his earlier position, McGlory restarted the pumping with the flat of his hands. This time each pressure he applied pushed more water out through Judy's mouth. Then there was no more to come.

Rolling her on to her side, checking that her tongue wasn't blocking her throat, McGlory knelt, cradling Judy in his lap. Rain still belted down so that he had to shelter her face by leaning a little forwards.

McGlory stayed like that for some time. He heard the lowing of cattle off in the night, and he wondered how far his herd had scattered. Kitty had crossed the river safely, he was sure of that. Sieber must have gone.

That solved a big problem, but not in the way McGlory would have wanted.

Unless Kitty had been able to cling onto the injured Baines, then he must have been washed out of the wagon. The tumble he had seen Clancy Magee take made it likely that the cook was dead. With the puncher named Tex that added up to probably four men lost on the river crossing. That was too many, despite the atrocious weather conditions.

Hearing Judy say just a single word surprised him. He couldn't be sure what she said, yet he felt good when her eyelids fluttered open. But her eyes widened in terror as she looked up at him. Opening her mouth, baring her upper teeth, Judy let loose a scream of horror that was all the more harrowing because it was silent. Then reason came back into her eyes. Judy sobbed for a few moments, then she looked at McGlory again and she was rational.

'I'm sorry, Joe. I was terrified when I woke up,' Judy said. 'You saved me.'

'Not really,' McGlory replied in a drawl. 'You were climbing up out of the river when I came along. I just helped you a little bit.'

Not believing a word, she managed to smile her thanks at him. She offered, 'I can make it back to the others now. I'm feeling pretty fit.'

Admiring her courage, McGlory told her to rest a while. When they did move it was slowly, and he supported her along the way. Soon McGlory could smell a fire up ahead and he crossed one of his dead off his mental list. The only man capable of getting a fire going with everything so wet was Clancy Magee.

But as they drew closer, McGlory put a finger to his lips for Judy to be silent. Leaning her against a tree, he signalled that he was leaving her for a little but would be back. She looked at him as he went, an expression of incredulity on her face that he could have heard anything in the blasting of wind and slashing rain.

McGlory moved off in an arc towards the fire of his own camp. Sensing something ahead of him, a person or an animal, he stopped. Carefully dividing some brush in front of his face, he saw a figure kneeling, looking into the camp. A rifle lay on the ground beside the man who, McGlory could see, was an Indian wearing a blue army uniform.

Totally unarmed, having lost the six-gun out of his holster and his knife from its sheath, McGlory inched carefully away, then hurried back to Judy. Relieved to see him, she reached out to put a hand on to his arm, which was all the support she now needed.

Close enough to the fire to be able to see the figures crouching round it, McGlory halted, ready to call out a warning that they were coming in, so that no one would panic and start shooting. But Luis beat him to it, startling those around him as well as Judy and McGlory by calling out, 'That you, Joe? Come on in.'

Kitty was on her feet, rushing to

embrace McGlory, sobbing, 'Thank God, Joe! Thank God! I was sure you were dead.'

Walking over in his bent-kneed, springingly lithe way, Luis shook McGlory by the hand. Head close to McGlory's ear he whispered a question. 'Did you check the *hombre* out there in the bushes?'

Giving a curt nod that answered the half-breed, McGlory had to blink as he saw Limm Sieber striding up to put a welcoming arm around Judy's shoulders. That was another one off the list. By some miracle Sieber had not perished.

'I'm right pleased by what you did for Judy, McGlory,' Sieber said, for a brief second looking as if he was going to extend his right hand, then withdrawing it. 'All the same, I want you to know that it won't alter what's between us.'

'I wouldn't expect it to, Sieber,' McGlory replied, then he kept one arm around Kitty and slapped Magee on the back with the other as the cook came hobbling up, massaging a sore neck.

'Lost most of the stuff, boss, victuals and the like,' Magee reported gloomily.

'Good thing,' a cowboy called from the fire. 'Give us a break from your danged cooking between here and Montana.'

There was some general laughter. That pleased McGlory. The men were in reasonably good spirits. The possibility of a revolt in the wake of the difficult crossing had occurred to him. He had a sudden thought!

'Anthom?' McGlory asked, peering round at the dark figures by the fire.

'I'm here, my good sir,' the Reverend Anthom boomed from the shadows. 'The good Lord didn't part the waters for us, but he got William, myself, and my wagon and worldly goods safely over the river.'

'You helped him, Luis,' McGlory made it a statement not a query, but the half-breed shook his head.

'None of us helped him, Joe,' Luis said, adding, apparently seriously, 'I reckon as how it must have been the Lord.'

'Then let's hope He's still around in the morning,' a cynical McGlory said irreverently, before raising his voice so that everyone there could hear. 'Dry out as best you can, men, and get yourself some sleep. We start the round-up soon as the sun shows. Preacher, you and William will ride with us. We're short handed now.'

He replied first with one of his poems. 'We reap, we sow in many lands, but not for the saintly toil with the hands.' Then he addressed McGlory sternly, 'I am not a gatherer of cattle, McGlory, but a gatherer of souls.'

'Cattle have souls, Preacher,' McGlory said in a weary voice, needing to dry out and re-arm himself before sleeping.

'I must object,' Anthom thundered. 'Cows do not have souls.'

'Mine will have at sun-up, Preacher,' McGlory replied laconically, 'so be there to start gathering.'

Taking his arm from around Kitty's waist, McGlory walked over to where Sieber was erecting a crude shelter for Judy to sleep under. An expression of curiosity on his face, the bounty hunter turned his head as McGlory approached.

'There's a Sioux brave out there in the brush, Sieber,' McGlory said softly. 'Reckon as how it'll mean something to you when I say he's wearing a blue army uniform.'

It was possible that Sieber's body tensed a little as he continued at his task, but he made no reply.

When McGlory was several paces from him, Sieber called, 'McGlory?'

Stopping but not turning even his head, McGlory waited.

'What made you tell me that?' Sieber asked.

Shrugging, McGlory answered, 'I guess I like to see a man, even the

217

kind of man you are, get an even break. Don't go and spoil a perfectly good relationship by thanking me, Sieber.'

'I don't intend to,' the bounty hunter said grimly.

As the night swallowed up Joe McGlory, his soft chuckle stayed behind, surviving alone for a little while.

9

Just days after the stormy river crossing, idyllic weather faded the memory of that struggle. It had taken less than three days to round up the scattered herd, and only a few head had been lost. McGlory had now reverted to making the drive by day, and everyone enjoyed a warm sun that didn't take the pureness out of the crisp autumn air. There was a splendour in the colours all around them, and it seemed that they had ridden out of a nightmare of terrible weather into some kind of paradise. The two women, and more than a few of the cowboys, appeared to have been lulled into a false belief that it would continue forever. Montana was just up ahead, nothing could go wrong.

But there was a strangeness to the sky that not only dimmed the light but gave it an unnatural hue. The air was dead and unmoving, and at night the moonlight was ghostly. McGlory and Luis had been watching the signs. The birds and wild geese had started south unusually early, and the willow brush had been stripped by beavers working in frantic anticipation of something. Also along the creeks that they passed the muskrats had constructed taller and thicker houses than was normal. They accepted that Sieber may well have noticed, but since the river crossing the bounty hunter had stayed closer to Judy while keeping himself separated from McGlory.

As he rode with Luis beside the wagons, McGlory heard the Reverend Anthom shout in his stentorian fashion, 'I am told there is an Episcopal church already built in Virginia City, Brother McGlory. No doubt when we reach there you will, in return for my joining you in a round-up of your cattle, unite with me in a praising of the Lord.'

'At least his intentions towards you

in Virginia City will be more civilized than those of Sieber,' Luis remarked wryly.

Had he been going to reply to either the preacher or the half-breed, McGlory would have been stopped by what he had seen out to his left. There on the range, far enough away from the herd to feel safe, were two white Arctic owls.

It was a bad sign and Luis and he exchanged worried glances. The odds against reaching Montana without encountering snow were shortening fast.

There was nothing to be done except push on as fast as possible. Baines had recovered enough from his injury to be able to ride drag. The cowboy still limped from the wrench his leg had received. He would probably be lame to some extent for the remainder of his life, but his contribution to the drive now was appreciated by McGlory. Since the near disaster with the chuckwagon in the water they had been short of food. The only meals

Clancy Magee could produce were meagre and boring. Yet the men were bearing up well in general, all of them fortified by the anticipation of a large pay-off in Montana. McGlory knew that Limm Sieber recognized this, and there would be no trouble from him until everything had been settled.

Moving his horse up to ride level with the buggy, McGlory told Kitty and Judy, 'Looks like some bad weather is mighty close.'

'Not more rain,' a worried Kitty sighed.

'Not this time. This time it will be snow, Kit,' McGlory said before dropping back to ride with Luis once more.

By the time the herd was pulled in, the night riders organized, and camp-fires had been lit, the only change had been a gradual but noticeable drop in temperature.

A little unnerved by the stillness, Kitty remarked, 'It's so quiet.'

'Make the most of it,' Luis warned

her as he brought in wood for McGlory's fire, a fire that the half-breed, by choice, would not be sitting beside.

Within an hour the temperature had plummeted below zero. The night herders found they had to raise their voices while crooning to soothe the cattle, for a wind had arisen. It came from the north-west to bring an end to the stillness of earth and sky that had held everyone in its spell. The sense of change was in itself disturbing.

What extra blankets had been saved crossing the river were distributed. Then a snow that was as fine as dust and as hard as grit was drifting in the wind. Deceptive in its fineness, it covered the range to a depth of six inches within a short time. Unused to it, the cattle from Texas became restless, wandering in aimless circles.

'Double the night watch,' McGlory instructed Grady, who was heading his way to ask what to do. 'The snow's got the beef on edge and it wouldn't take much to spook them.'

Agreeing, Grady hurried off to arouse grumbling punchers who were already in their bedrolls. A stampede was likely. Everyone needed to be alert.

'What does this mean, Joe?' an anxious Kitty asked, and Judy, who had been joined by Sieber, awaited McGlory's answer worriedly.

'If it eases down, then we'll be fine,' McGlory replied. 'But if this is the start of a long, hard winter, then the beef won't survive.'

'It will all have been for nothing,' Kitty said, so softly that those around her knew that she was talking to herself.

'How do you see it, Luis?' McGlory asked the half-breed, who was taking food from Magee, ready to go off to eat alone.

Peering at the snow, reaching out to capture some of the small, hard flakes to test them between his fingers, the 'breed then held his face into the wind before answering. 'It could get worse overnight, Joe, but then I think we'll have enough good weather to see us into Montana.'

This good news made the sparse meal enjoyable, but the drifting snow had even the exuberant Reverend Anthom subdued. But when everyone had eaten and was moving away from the fire, he came up to speak to McGlory in a confidential whisper.

'Our fellow traveller has been asking questions, Joe,' the preacher said.

'Sieber?'

'Yes,' a grave-faced Anthom nodded. 'He wants to know about the burnt sacrifice, as it were; who the man was.'

Looking questioningly at Anthom, McGlory said, 'And, as an honest man of God, you had to tell him, Preacher.'

'You misjudge me, brother.' The preacher looked hurt. 'As I have no idea of the name of the person concerned, my integrity was not in any way compromised. However, I do know *what* the man was, and you would be well advised to tell Brother Sieber. I feel that to do so would mercifully save the lives of one or both of you.'

'I don't have to explain myself to any man, Preacher,' McGlory said dully, just finishing his sentence as the sound of a rifle shot exploded in the night air.

A running McGlory was joined by Luis. They reached where Sieber and Judy had been standing close. Sieber had been setting up the woman's lean-to shelter against the side of the chuckwagon, when a shot had knocked Judy off her feet. She lay flat on her face, blood running from her upper body to stain the snow dark red. Sieber was down on one knee at her side. It was clear what had happened. The Sioux in the army uniform had fired from the security of darkness. Either he had missed Sieber or was building his campaign of hate by deliberately shooting the bounty hunter's woman first.

Although concerned for the woman,

McGlory was listening to the noise the cattle were making. Aware of the importance of keeping the herd calm, the night riders couldn't disguise the alarm in their voices. The rifle shot had wound up the herd as tight as a spring. One foolish move by a man or a horse, or maybe just the scuttling passage of a creature of the night, and that spring would snap suddenly.

'Take care of her, Kitty,' Sieber said with a nod at the prone Judy as Kitty came hurrying up.

Having said this, Sieber stood, reaching for where he had leant his rifle against the wheel of the wagon. Moving fast, McGlory snaked out a foot to send the rifle falling into the snow. He was carrying his own Remington, and it was now carelessly half aimed at Sieber.

'Where do you think you're going, Sieber?' McGlory asked.

'After that Sioux. He's been smarting since me'n him had that fight a while back.'

'There's more to it than that, Sieber,'

Luis said. 'He's been after you for a long time. The way I hear it you collected bounty on one of his kin.'

'If I did he was guilty,' Sieber grunted, bending to put a hand out for his rifle, but McGlory kicked it a little further away.

'Don't push it too far, McGlory,' Sieber cautioned nastily, watching from the corner of his eye as Kitty and Clancy Magee gently picked up Judy and carried her away.

'I'll push it just as far as I have to, Sieber,' McGlory said evenly. 'I want every man out there circling the herd. We can't risk another stampede.'

'The snow will have covered that redskin's tracks,' Sieber protested.

Squinting up into the dark sky, Luis observed, 'The snow will have covered his tracks in about two minutes, Sieber.'

'You help us tonight, Sieber,' McGlory looked steadily at the bounty hunter, 'and we'll help you get that Sioux in the morning.'

Reaching down, McGlory picked up Sieber's rifle with one hand and threw it to him, lowering his own rifle as Sieber caught his. The invitation was there, a metaphorical gauntlet had been thrown down, and for a moment it seemed that Sieber would pick it up. Hefting the rifle, he stared angrily at McGlory. Then Sieber lowered his rifle and made his way towards the horses, followed by Luis and McGlory.

An hour later, with all hands having ridden a steady circle around the herd, singing mournful, cow-sedating songs, and calling softly and comfortingly to the animals, the threat of a stampede had receded.

'I guess it's all over for tonight, boss,' Grady reported when riding up to McGlory.

'Put fresh herders on, Grady, then stand the rest of the men down,' McGlory ordered as he watched Luis approaching.

'Sieber's gone,' the half-breed said. 'Could be he lit out some time ago.'

'Probably did,' McGlory answered, uninterested now that the immediate danger of a stampede had passed.

He rode back into camp then, only shrugging and not speaking when Luis asked, 'Do we go hunting for him in the morning?'

Looking for Kitty he found her nursing Judy in the chuckwagon. The bullet had hit Judy in the shoulder. It had gone clear through, not hitting any bones or doing any permanent damage. She was conscious, her face white as she enquired after Sieber.

'He's gone after the Sioux who did the shooting,' McGlory told her, watching anxiety crease her face.

'Will you go help Limm, Joe?' Judy asked plaintively.

Not answering her, McGlory stepped down off the wagon and was about to walk off into the night when he heard Kitty scrambling down to the ground behind him.

'Will you go after him, Joe?' she asked in a whisper.

'You mean go get Sieber back so he won't miss the chance to kill me when we reach Montana?' he asked bitterly.

'I want him back for Judy's sake, Joe,' Kitty said quietly. 'He's all she's got now, the only thing to cling on to. She was telling me about herself when I was taking care of her wound. She had a homestead, Joe, a husband and three little ones — a boy and two girls. Some renegade Sioux hit their settlement one night. They killed her husband and children, Joe. They took her, but some young bucks got to fighting about who she belonged to, and she was able to run off while the fight was going on. Sieber found her and he's been taking care of her ever since.'

Listening to what Kitty was saying, McGlory walked away without a word when she had finished speaking.

In the morning, with the snow having ceased, though the temperature was still below zero, there was a promise that the sun might shine later. Luis had been right about the weather, and

231

now McGlory had another question for him.

'How do you reckon Sieber's chances out there, Luis?'

Thoughtful for a moment, the half-breed then said, 'If he's up against just the brave in the soldier's suit, Joe, then Sieber will take care of him. But if there's more hostiles around, and I'm mighty sure there are, then Sieber ain't likely to come back.'

'I'm thinking of getting Grady moving with the herd, then going out to take a look for Sieber,' McGlory said.

'I'll be ready to ride out with you, Joe.'

'I didn't ask you to side me, Luis.'

'You didn't have to, you knew I'd tag along.' The half-breed gave him a grin.

Later, when McGlory had given Grady his instructions, and he and Luis were riding away, the latter asked, 'Do you miss the wild days, Joe?'

'I suppose I do,' McGlory acknowledged. 'It's taking longer to bury

Apache Joe than I thought it would, much longer.'

'I kind of guessed that. At times you look the part, just like a young Jesse Chisholm,' Luis said; the only time he was ever free with words was when he was with McGlory. 'Then something happens and you change right back into Apache Joe.'

'The Apache bit ain't natural with me, Luis. I'm slowly getting rid of it.'

'If it don't work, Joe, we can always go back,' the half-breed said hopefully.

'I'm never going back,' McGlory was adamant, and he didn't speak again until they came upon Limm Sieber.

They didn't exactly come upon him. They were riding along a ridge that led to a sloping ledge. No more than six feet wide, it had been turned into a glacier by snow and the freezing temperature. Below the ledge was a sheer drop down into the rocky, snow and ice-covered bottom of a canyon. Rising up from the ledge was an icy slope of some sixty feet. To attempt to go mounted or on foot along the ledge would mean a certain slip to the canyon floor far below. They had reined in when Luis's keen eyes spotted something down in the canyon. He pointed it out to McGlory, and by studying the dark blob they eventually agreed that it was the shattered body of an Indian dressed in blue army uniform. Less than a second later they caught sight of Sieber.

In a precarious position some thirty yards along the ledge from McGlory and Luis, the bounty hunter must have slipped during a fight to the death, probably in the dark, with the Sioux who had been trailing him. Now he lay face down across a projection of rock that was six feet below the ledge. There was no way that Sieber could climb back up on to the ledge. Even if he could manage it, the sloping sheet of ice would cause him to slide off and fall to his death.

Taking their lariats with them as they dismounted, McGlory and Luis climbed a little way up the bank above the ledge. Then, with McGlory leading, they worked their way along the bank, using every available foot and handhold. As they went they unrolled the lariat, fixing it behind rocks, tying it where possible, making sure that they had something to cling on to on the return climb. It was difficult going. The icy conditions froze their hands even inside of their gloves, and their feet slipped often.

At last they were above Sieber. Selecting a spur, they fastened the end of the second lariat to it, letting the rope drop down. The end dangled about six feet below where the bounty hunter lay.

McGlory went down the rope then. Reaching the ledge his feet went out from under him immediately. Slipping at speed, he was dangling out over the edge, maintaining a hold on the rope with one hand.

With a worried Luis watching him from above, McGlory swung his body out into space to give himself the momentum to throw his arm upwards and grasp the rope with his second hand. Pausing to rest for a while, feeling pain from where his body had smashed against the side of the canyon, he lowered himself down.

There was just room for McGlory to place both of his feet on the projection of rock. He got one of his feet in close to the face of the cliff, and the other out between Sieber's legs. It meant that McGlory was standing astride, but he had no alternative. The problem was how to get the bounty hunter back up to where Luis waited. If he tied the rope around Sieber, then Luis wouldn't have the strength to pull the man up, particularly as the half-breed had only a poor footing that forced him to keep his back against the bank to avoid falling.

He was bending, holding on to the rope with one end as he struggled to get the end of the rope under Sieber's middle without dislodging him, when the bounty hunter turned his head to look up at him. Sieber's face had been turned purple by the cold, and when he spoke his voice seemed to have to struggle to come up from somewhere deep in the depths of him.

'Secure me with the rope so that I can move my arms and legs to get life back into them,' Sieber asked.

Keenly aware what agony this would cause the bounty hunter, McGlory fumblingly obeyed, but he had a word of caution. 'Move too much, Sieber, and you'll have us both at the bottom of the canyon.'

'Trust me,' Sieber said, wriggling his fingers, then moving his arms and legs, sweat breaking out on his brow despite the freezing conditions. 'Give 'em a couple of minutes and I'll be able to climb up the rope.'

McGlory doubted Sieber, despite the confidence he showed. The bounty hunter must have been lying across that rock, suspended over the canyon in sub-zero temperatures for many hours. Having stayed alive was a feat: climbing up the rope would be a miracle.

But it was a miracle that Sieber performed. Both of them moved carefully on the projecting rock, the bounty hunter safer because the rope was tied around his middle. Then, holding on with one hand, he untied the rope and together he and McGlory tied it round McGlory's waist. As agile as a monkey, defying all logic with a display of strength and mobility after such an experience, he went hand over hand up the rope.

Slithering and sliding, the bounty hunter cleared the icy ledge. He climbed a couple of feet up the bank then, below Luis, and waited for McGlory to start climbing.

When his head was just below the ledge, McGlory's face was slashed by splinters of rock and shards of ice as a bullet struck the cliff face beside his head. He heard two more shots fired from the far side of the canyon, and guessed there were Sioux over there. One bullet slapped into the ice harmlessly above his head, but he felt the second bullet tug at his left boot. He felt the warmth of blood flowing from his cold foot inside the boot.

Bracing himself for further shooting, McGlory heard a sporadic fusillade fired, but no bullets came his way. Looking up he saw Luis swinging along the rope fast. Hand over hand, the half-breed was heading back towards where they had left their horses. He was drawing fire. Able to see bullets ripping into the rock and ice close to Luis, McGlory didn't think it possible that the 'breed could make it without being hit.

Reaching the end of the rope, still under fire from at least three rifles, Luis leapt down to land on his feet beside the horses. Pulling his Remington rifle clear, he returned fire across the canyon.

Then there was silence once more. Replacing his rifle, Luis came back along the rope to meet Sieber and McGlory as they climbed up.

'There were three of them,' Luis said. 'I got 'em all, but I'm only sure that two are dead. The last one might cause us more trouble.'

But there were no more shots. With McGlory bringing up the rear, untying the lariat as he moved along the bank, they got back to the horses. Having regained his natural complexion, Sieber appeared to be totally unaffected by the ordeal he had been through. He looked more like a man who had spent a night in a comfortable bed, than he did someone who had been inches from death.

'You double up on Luis's horse,' McGlory told him, 'and we'll ride back steady.'

'No need. I left my horse over there behind those junipers,' the bounty hunter said, walking off, as steady as the frozen rocks he was walking on.

Watching Sieber go, Luis commented appreciatively, 'There goes one hard man, Joe.'

'You're right,' McGlory nodded. 'I'd

rather he was for me than against me.'

'He could well be now,' Luis suggested, his implication being that Sieber would be grateful to McGlory for saving his life.

'Not a chance, Luis,' McGlory shook his head. 'Men like Limm Sieber are single-minded. What has happened here will mean nothing to him when he calls me out when we reach Montana.'

'Maybe you should have left him dangling off that rock, Joe.'

'Maybe I should have,' a grim-faced McGlory agreed.

10

'You've got yourself a deal, McGlory,' Max Harmmis, Virginia City's best-known businessman said, shaking McGlory by the hand. 'Now, bring your lovely lady with you and we'll drink to our future.'

They were in the Capitol Hotel, initially as honoured guests having made the trail drive from Texas, and now as business partners. In building a permanent corral outside of the city, McGlory had achieved what he had set out to do, by establishing Texas cattle ranching in Montana. Harmmis had liked his ambition, his determination, and his style, and had immediately offered to join McGlory's venture at the Montana end. As he poured drinks for Kitty, McGlory and himself in the lounge of the plush hotel, Max Harmmis smiled affably at them both.

'You'll find me to be a straight dealer, McGlory,' Harmmis said. 'I wouldn't dream of robbing you of one red cent.'

'If you did I'd kill you,' McGlory said, soft-voiced, and Harmmis laughed heartily until he realized it wasn't a joke.

Face serious, showing a little fear, Harmmis, for a reason best known to himself, apologized. 'Forgive me, McGlory, forgive me. I'm unaccustomed to doing business with men like yourself.'

'I'm not accustomed to being in the company of men like yourself.' McGlory used words that could be taken either as a statement of fact or an insult. Harmmis wisely accepted it as the former.

'How do you see things from now on, McGlory?' the businessman asked. 'What are your plans?'

'Kitty and myself will be going back down the trail to fetch up another herd,' McGlory replied. 'In the meantime I'll be leaving a man here to take care of things.'

It was the second arrangement that worried McGlory. The Indian in Luis meant that he couldn't stay in one place for long, so McGlory couldn't leave him in Montana. Grady was a good man out on the trail, but he didn't have the brains to run an operation such as McGlory had planned for here. This problem had occupied his mind most of the time, to the frustration of Kitty who was constantly worrying over Sieber, and persisted in trying to force McGlory into a firm decision on the threat posed by the bounty hunter.

Although he didn't confess it to Kitty, Sieber had been a worry that never ceased niggling at the back of Joe's mind. Proud of having changed himself from the renegade Apache Joe to the cattle baron Joe McGlory, he wanted to build on his achievements. But the shadow of Limm Sieber fell across every design and hope McGlory had for the future. Not afraid to face the bounty hunter, McGlory had no illusions. Sieber was a formidable adversary. Confident that he could beat any other man that he knew, McGlory didn't argue when common sense told him that he could possibly have met his match in Sieber.

Soon after they had got to Virginia City, the Reverend Lionel Anthom had left to join his church, and William had gone off eagerly to organize his hanging. Luis had stayed with the cattle and the men, because the 'breed had nowhere else to go, and Sieber, still attentive to the injured Judy, hung around broodily, rarely moving far enough away from McGlory to lose sight of him.

'We'll finish our drink and then go to the bank,' Harmmis said. 'I'll make my payment to you in cash, McGlory.'

'That's the way I want it,' McGlory said.

When he had the cash, McGlory placed most of it in the safe at the rear of the saloon that Harmmiss owned. Then he rode back to the camp with

Kitty and called the men together.

'This is the end of the drive,' McGlory addressed the cowpunchers, 'but it needn't be the end of us working together. I'll be paying you off tonight, but any man among you who wants to can go back down to Texas with us to start another drive.'

'You can count me in,' Clancy Magee shouted.

'Then count us out if he's going to be cook again,' a cowboy called amid a lot of laughter.

Luis had come over to stand at McGlory's side, and McGlory called to the man who he had made his foreman. 'What about you, Grady?'

'I'm with you, boss,' Grady replied.

Standing beside Judy, whose arm was in a sling, Sieber said nothing. McGlory continued, 'I won't ask any of you boys to decide now. You get your pay, then have your fun, then tell me whether you want to ride with me again. I'll pay you out tonight at the

Buckhorn Saloon. Will you be there, Sieber?'

'I'll be there,' Sieber said in a way that could have been a promise, but was most likely a threat.

* * *

Judge Wade Percival's office was not impressive. Squeezed in between a barber's shop and a carpenter's premises where the main trade was in coffins, it had the look of a derelict seed store, and smelled heavily of alcohol. The judge himself had the bleary-eyed look of the town drunk, but was saved from such a classification by the expensive clothes that he wore. Two years ago the distress on Percival's face had been caused by a stone in the kidney. He had started drinking to kill the pain, and now not even he could separate the effects of the stone from the symptoms caused by alcohol. He hadn't stood when Limm Sieber had walked in, and was muttering grumpily now as he sorted through a mess of papers on his desk.

'Ah, here we are,' he said with a grunt of satisfaction, then fell quiet to read the paper he had picked up. Turning to Sieber, annoyance added to everything else that was registered on his worn face, he said accusingly, 'You are wasting my time, young man. Apache Joe died in a fire just hours before he was due to hang. No, not hours. It says here that it was no more than a matter of minutes.'

Sieber sat on the corner of the deck, but came upright again as the judge glared angrily at him. Percival's eyes took in the oiled holster, the worn handle of Sieber's gun, then looked back up at his face in anticipation of an explanation.

'That isn't true what it says there,' Sieber told him. 'The man who died in the fire was not Apache Joe. He escaped, Judge.'

With suspicion half-closing his blood-shot eyes, Percival asked, 'Are you a lawman of some kind?'

'Not exactly,' Sieber replied.

'Ah!' the judge exclaimed as he found his answer. 'Bounty hunter, eh?'

Sieber answered with a nod.

'Well, Mr Bounty Hunter . . . '

'The name's Sieber, Judge,' Sieber said.

'What's in a name, Sieber?' Percival said, with a shrug of his thin shoulders. 'The thing is, whatever you said your name was, you made a mistake in coming here looking to get paid out for a renegade who died long ago.'

'Apache Joe didn't die,' Sieber coldly insisted.

'Proof?' The Judge lifted both eyebrows to lay stress on his question. 'You can give me proof of this, Sieber?'

'I can do better than that, Judge. I can give you Apache Joe.'

'Now look here, young man,' Percival became sternly angry. 'I don't take kindly to boasters, and it seems to me you're doing one mighty big heap of boasting.'

'I'm telling you the truth, Judge, not

boasting,' Sieber said. 'I'll be in the Buckhorn Saloon tonight and I'll give you Apache Joe.'

'Dead or alive?' Percival asked nervously.

'That will depend on Apache Joe, Judge.'

Sitting for a few minutes in quiet contemplation, Percival then wagged a gnarled finger at Sieber. 'I'll be there, Sieber. I'll be bringing a team of law officers with me, so you'd better be telling the truth, young man. I said a minute or two ago that I don't take kindly to boasting. Well, how I feel about boasting don't mean a cow's cuss compared to how I get if anyone tries to make a fool of me.'

'I'm not the sort of man who goes in for fooling, Judge,' Sieber said as he walked towards the door. 'Come alone if that suits you. I can take care of Apache Joe.'

★ ★ ★

250

The church building was without charm, but the aspirations of its designers were in evidence. With better days to come in mind, provisions had been made for a spire to be added on, and the upright oblong windows had been let into the walls in a way that would easily allow them to be topped by arches later. As Kitty and Judy approached they read a bold-lettered sign outside: BAPTISTS, METHODISTS, LUTHERANS, AND THE REST OF YOU SINNERS ARE WELCOME AT THE LORD'S TABLE.

Still caught up in the excitement of finding himself in charge of a permanent church, the Reverend Lionel Anthom didn't seem to quite have a grasp of what was going on around him. He greeted the two women politely enough, but it was as if he had met them just once, briefly and a long time ago. It wasn't until Kitty introduced the subject that had brought them there, that he fully realized who they were.

'My dear child.' He shook a sad

head. 'I have done all that the Almighty could expect of me in this direction. In the case of McGlory it is a matter of pride coming before the fall. I have pleaded with him, and prayed to God, asking no more than McGlory speak to Sieber, thereby averting what is sure to be a tragedy.'

'Joe will not be moved,' Kitty agreed unhappily.

'It is a terrible thing,' Anthom declared, 'because there is so much opportunity here in Montana, a state which needs men of vision such as McGlory.' He turned to Judy. 'What about you, my child, cannot you bring influence to bear on Sieber? He has spoken to me of making you his wife before God. Perhaps if you made his abandonment of his act of vengeance against McGlory a condition of your agreeing to marry him?'

'I've tried that,' Judy said glumly.

'But you, Kitty, it was yourself who recruited me to rescue Apache Joe from the gallows,' the preacher said. 'You were there. You know exactly what took place. You could explain it all to Sieber.'

'As could you, Reverend,' Kitty replied. 'You know every bit as much as I do.'

'McGlory has forbidden me to say a word, and as a man of God I have a duty to respect his wishes.'

With a wry smile, Kitty said, 'As his wife I have a much greater duty to Joe.'

Accepting this with a nod, Anthom sighed. 'They are two dangerous men about to collide head on for no good reason.'

'They have a reason that means everything to them, Preacher,' Judy said. 'It is their pride. Limm has told me that Joe is the only man he ever went out after and didn't bring back.'

'So be it,' Anthom said resignedly. 'We can do nothing but wait, my children. When it has all been settled, Judy, I will marry you to your man.'

'What if he is dead?' a mournful Judy questioned.

'Then,' Anthom told her sombrely, 'I will see that he gets a Christian burial.'

When they had left the church, Judy asked, 'Is there anything else we can do, Kitty?'

'No,' Kitty replied flatly. 'Like the preacher said, Judy, all we can do is wait.'

★ ★ ★

All day William had toiled. Now as evening settled in on the city, folk came up to study his creation. It was a perfect machine, a smoothly working gallows that he tested over and over again with pride for every group of visitors. It was well known that he was there to execute one Billy Bartley, an alcoholic who had stabbed his wife to death in the street. Bartley had been sentenced to death by Judge Percival. William, appointed by Washington to

254

dispense convicted killers into the next world, was there to send Bartley off as comfortably as possible.

'My work has brought testimonials from the nether regions,' William boasted, resting one hand on his hanging machine. As always when doing a public appearance, William's snowy-white shirt was ornamented by a large diamond. 'It is a misnomer to call me a hangman. I am the master of ceremonies at every execution. My work is in great demand, folks. Yet even I can not be in two parts of the country at the same time. Consequently, the condemned ones all over the country have to wait on my convenience.'

Watching and listening from a short distance away, Limm Sieber walked over when there was a lull in the flow of sightseers to the gallows. William acknowledged his arrival with a welcoming nod and, eager to go on boasting, studied Sieber in an attempt at gauging if the bounty hunter would be receptive to his patter. But Sieber spoke first.

'They did you out of the hanging of Apache Joe,' Sieber said, feigning sympathy to draw William out on the subject.

The hangman's answer surprised him. 'That was one I didn't mind losing.'

'The way I hear it, it was a bad business,' Sieber insisted. 'Some poor guy getting roasted in Apache Joe's place.'

'That was an example of master planning,' William smiled in fond reminiscence, 'and I am most pleased to have had a hand in it.'

Sieber prompted, 'It must have been good to fool a man like Phil Comber.'

'It wasn't anything to do with the sheriff,' William chuckled. 'It was young Arthur Greening, the deputy, that the Reverend Anthom and Miss Kitty got to let them bring that fella in while Comber was at breakfast.'

'Who knifed the man in the jail?'

Sieber tersely enquired.

'Joe, of course. The Reverend gave them both knives and left them to it. It was all fair and above board. Apache Joe won, like we all thought he would.'

While aware that William was speaking the truth, Sieber had difficulty in accepting that either Anthom or Kitty would be involved in such murderous subterfuge, and he expressed his misgivings to the hangman.

'Reverend Anthom's an Old Testament preacher, sir, 'an eye for eye, a tooth for a tooth', that's his creed,' William smiled. 'The reverend and Kitty knew as well as we all did that the fella who got burned deserved to die. There were three of them, see, not two like everyone thinks.'

'Three of who?' Sieber couldn't follow the hangman's turn of conversation.

'Those who attacked and murdered Apache Joe's sister,' William replied. 'That was the third man who was killed in the jail by Joe. Good riddance to him is what we all say.'

The hangman wasn't sure that Sieber, who was walking away, had heard his last few words.

* ★ ★

There was a tension in the Buckhorn Saloon that was continuing to build. McGlory was aware of it, but couldn't be bothered to give thought to what it was. He had paid off his men, who were now getting drunk fast and letting off steam. All of them but Sieber had been paid. The bounty hunter had not put in an appearance. That could be the cause of the tension, McGlory thought in a detached way. Maybe it was just him feeling it. This hadn't occurred to him before, but he realized that he had wanted Sieber to come at him, to get it over with.

Leaning close, talking secretively to McGlory as he refilled his glass with whiskey, Max Harmmis asked, 'Do you see that strange-looking guy in the top hat, sitting by the piano?'

The place wasn't crowded, and McGlory took a covert look to spot a middle-aged man with a drink-flushed complexion. He confirmed his sighting for Harmmis. 'I see him.'

'That's Judge Percival,' Harmmis informed McGlory. 'He's got the law in this city, such as it is, in his pocket. A few of us have got through to Washington, and we've been assured that a US Marshal will be coming down to establish a proper law system in Virginia City. But my guess is that we've got a long wait. Until then we're stuck with Percival.'

'Does that worry you?' McGlory enquired, the greater part of his mind on other things.

Harmmis's whisper was a hoarse one. 'I reckon as how it's you that should be worried, McGlory. There's Percival's men spread out in here tonight. They are gunmen not lawmen, McGlory, and the judge is up to something.'

'Why should that concern me, Harmmis?'

'Well,' Harmmis sorted out his words as he spoke. 'Apart from your trail hands, who don't count, you're the only stranger in here tonight, McGlory. Stands to reason that it's you Percival's got in his sights.'

'Why?' McGlory asked.

'Beats me,' Harmmis answered, and tipped a full glass of whiskey down his throat as Limm Sieber came in the door.

Not looking in Sieber's direction, McGlory was nevertheless aware that the bounty hunter was walking slowly towards him. Adjusting his stance, keeping one elbow on the bar, McGlory eased his right hip out a little so that his six-gun was readily accessible. He looked up when he heard Sieber stop a few feet from him.

'You're the only man who'll ever hear me say this, McGlory, but I admit I was wrong,' Sieber said.

The bounty hunter had turned and

was walking to the door. Bewildered, McGlory was trying to work out what had happened when he saw Judge Percival get up out of his chair and stride over swiftly to block Sieber's way. Two hard-faced gunslingers had moved to stand behind the bounty hunter.

'Where's Apache Joe, Sieber?' Percival asked, his manner threatening.

'I heard tell he died in a fire just before they were going to hang him,' Sieber replied in a relaxed, easy way.

Jerking his head forwards, turtle-like, the judge said in a hissing voice, 'I warned you that I won't be fooled with, Sieber.'

The alert McGlory saw Harmmis signal to his barman. Surreptitiously, the barman, a lanky man with a loosely hanging bottom lip and a projecting Adam's apple, brought a double-barrelled shotgun up from under the bar.

To his right, McGlory saw a man with his back against a wall and a clear line between Sieber and himself, start to draw. Clearing his own holster fast, McGlory fired to blast a blood-pumping hole in the gunman's chest.

Springing into action, Sieber elbowed Percival to one side, sending the judge staggering, and drew his gun at the same time. But a man who had been unobtrusively playing cards across a table with a second man, jumped to his feet to swing a chair by its back and knock Sieber's gun from his hand with it.

The two men who had been standing behind Sieber were drawing their guns. Firing, hitting one of them in the back so that his top half fell backwards when the bullet smashed his spine in two, McGlory reached with his left hand to snatch the shotgun from the barman.

'Sieber!' McGlory shouted, hurtling the shotgun through the air to the bounty hunter.

Catching the weapon, Sieber used its butt to smash in the face of the second gunman who was close to him.

As that man thudded to the floor, Sieber fired one barrel to make a bloody mash of the face and body of a man who had been levelling a six-gun at him. A gunman who had turned a round table on its side and was about to seek cover behind it, was the target for Sieber's second barrel. Blasted backwards, hands going up above his head as he hit the wall, the gunman fell dead as McGlory shot a man who had been up on a small balcony, taking a steady bead on Sieber.

In slow motion the man toppled over a low balustrade to plummet down smashing a table and several glasses as he landed.

All was very still and quiet then, as if the sudden burst of action had been too much and now everyone was frozen into stillness. A crazy kind of laugh broke the silence. It had been uttered by a man with the look of an idiot. Wearing a *poncho*, his gait was lame and there was a foolish grin on his face as he limped up to where the bleeding, broken body that had fallen from the balcony lay.

'Who bin dooding all de shooting?' the grinning fool inanely enquired.

'Shoot him, McGlory,' Harmmis whispered urgently. 'Cut him down.'

Not even certain that Harmmis had been referring to the idiot, McGlory had no intention of shooting such a pathetic creature. With a quick glance round the bar, confident that there was no further danger, McGlory let his gun slip easily back into its holster.

'McGlory!' Harmmis cried, looking for the shotgun that was no longer with his barman.

The insistence in the businessman's voice alerted McGlory, and then he noticed the slight movement under the *poncho* worn by the idiot. Drawing, McGlory fired a split second before a hole was burnt into the *poncho* and a bullet fired by the crippled man splintered the wood of the bar an inch from McGlory's side.

The shock at the idiot being armed and one of the judge's men had made McGlory's shooting slightly inaccurate. His bullet tore off the idiot's left ear with a clump of red hair attached to it. Brown, black, and yellow-pointed teeth bared in extreme agony, the idiot did a frantically mad dance. Everyone in the saloon watched spellbound as he spun and leapt about this way and that, knocking against tables, jumping up and down, the left side of his head and face exposed in a gruesome fashion.

Not wanting to fire again, McGlory was thinking he would have to in order to put the idiot out of his misery, when the dance ended and the crippled man dropped dead on to the floor.

Somewhere in the saloon someone let out a mighty guffaw that was silenced part way through. It was very quiet again then until Judge Percival, who had been standing close to Sieber, his face ashen, started to run. He was coming away from Sieber, and McGlory moved to intercept him.

Catching Percival by the arm, McGlory swung the judge round so that he was facing Sieber. Raising a leg to place a foot in the centre of Percival's back, McGlory propelled him towards the bounty hunter at speed.

As the judge came towards him, Sieber held the shotgun barrels with both hands and brought it up viciously into Percival's groin. As a scream of total suffering was ripped out of Percival, Sieber brought up the gun to swing it sideways so that when it connected with the judge's head it seemed it would rip it from his shoulders.

Throwing the gun down on top of the judge, Sieber took one look around before walking to the door. McGlory, needing to clear his throat because of the acrid stench of gunsmoke, said to Harmmis, 'I guess that's fixed one of your problems with the law in Virginia City.'

Then McGlory went out into the street. Standing in the shadows of the saloon, he reloaded his gun. Putting it back into its holster he walked out to see Sieber standing in the middle of the street, waiting for him.

Walking a little closer to the bounty hunter, hand hovering over his six-gun, McGlory stopped and asked, 'Something on your mind, Sieber?'

'Yes,' Sieber answered coolly. 'I hear you're looking for someone to take care of business this end.'

'I reckon as how I've found him,' McGlory said.

The two men closed the distance between them then, and shook each other by the hand.

THE END

THE CROOKED SHERIFF
John Dyson

Black Pete Bowen quit Texas with a burning hatred of men who try to take the law into their own hands. But he discovers that things aren't much different in the silver mountains of Arizona.

THEY'LL HANG BILLY
FOR SURE:
Larry & Stretch
Marshall Grover

Billy Reese, the West's most notorious desperado, was to stand trial. From all compass points came the curious and the greedy, the riff-raff of the frontier. Suddenly, a crazed killer was on the loose — but the Texas Trouble-Shooters were there, girding their loins for action.

RIDERS OF RIFLE RANGE
Wade Hamilton

Veterinarian Jeff Jones did not like open warfare — but it was there on Scrub Pine grass. When he diagnosed a sick bull on the Endicott ranch as having the contagious blackleg disease, he got involved in the warfare — whether he liked it or not!

BEAR PAW
Nevada Carter

Austin Dailey traded two cows to a pair of Indians for a bay horse, which subsequently disappeared. Tracks led to a secret hideout of fugitive Indians — and cattle thieves. Indians and stockmen co-operated against the rustlers. But it was Pale Woman who acted as interpreter between her people and the rangemen.

THE WEST WITCH
Lance Howard

Detective Quinton Hilcrest journeys west, seeking the Black Hood Bandits' lost fortune. Within hours of arriving in Hags Bend, he is fighting for his life, ensnared with a beautiful outcast the town claims is a witch! Can he save the young woman from the angry mob?

GUNS OF THE PONY EXPRESS
T. M. Dolan

Rich Zennor joined the Pony Express venture at the start, as second-in-command to tough Denning Hartman. But Zennor had the problems of Hartman believing that they had crossed trails in the past, and the fact that he was strongly attached to Hartman's Indian girl, Conchita.

BLACK JO OF THE PECOS
Jeff Blaine

Nobody knew where Black Josephine Callard came from or whither she returned. Deputy U.S. Marshal Frank Haggard would have to exercise all his cunning and ability to stay alive before he could defeat her highly successful gang and solve the mystery.

RIDE FOR YOUR LIFE
Johnny Mack Bride

They rode west, hoping for a new start. Then they met another broken-down casualty of war, and he had a plan that might deliver them from despair. But the only men who would attempt it would be the truly brave — or the desperate. They were both.

THE NIGHTHAWK
Charles Burnham

While John Baxter sat looking at the ruin that arsonists had made of his log house, a stranger rode into the yard. Baxter and Walt Showalter partnered up and re-built the house. But when it was dynamited, they struck back — and all hell broke loose.

MAVERICK PREACHER
M. Duggan

Clay Purnell was hopeful that his posting to Capra would be peaceable enough. However, on his very first day in town he rode into trouble. Although loath to use his .45, Clay found he had little choice — and his likeness to a notorious bank robber didn't help either!

SIXGUN SHOWDOWN
Art Flynn

After years as a lawman elsewhere, Dan Herrick returned to his old Arizona stamping ground to find that nesters were being driven from their homesteads by ruthless ranchers. Before putting away his gun once and for all, Dan forced a bloody and decisive showdown.

RIDE LIKE THE DEVIL!
Sam Gort

Ben Trunch arrived back on the Big T only to find that land-grabbing was in progress. He confronted Luke Fletcher, saloon-keeper and town boss, with what was happening, and was immediately forced to ride for his life. But he got the chance to put it all right in the end.

SLOW WOLF AND DAN FOX:
Larry & Stretch
Marshall Grover

The deck was stacked against an innocent man. Larry Valentine played detective, and his investigation propelled the Texas Trouble-Shooters into a gun-blazing fight to the finish.

BRANAGAN'S LAW
Alan Irwin

To Angus Flint, the valley was his domain and he didn't want any new settlers. But Texas Ranger Jim Branagan had other ideas. Could he put an end to Flint's tyranny for good?

THE DEVIL RODE A PINTO
Bret Rey

When a settler is cut to ribbons in a frenzied attack, Texas Ranger Sam Buck learns that the killer is Rufus Berry, known as The Devil. Sam stiffens his resolve to kill or capture Berry and break up his gang.

THE DEATH MAN
Lee F. Gregson

The hardest of men went in fear of Ford, the bounty hunter, who had earned the name 'The Death Man'. Yet even Ford was not infallible — when he killed the wrong man, he found that he was being sought himself by the feared Frank Ambler.

LEAD LANGUAGE
Gene Tuttle

After Blaze Colton and Ricky Rawlings have delivered a train load of cows from Arizona to San Francisco, they become involved in a load of trouble and find themselves on the run!

A DOLLAR FROM THE STAGE
Bill Morrison

Young saddle-tramp Len Finch stumbled into a web of murder, lawlessness, intrigue and evil ambition. In the end, he put his life on the line for the folks that he cared about.

BRAND 2: HARDCASE
Neil Hunter

When Ben Wyatt and his gang hold up the bank in Adobe, Wyatt is captured. Judge Rice asks Jason Brand, an ex-U.S. Marshal, to take up the silver star. Wyatt is in the cells, his men close by, and Brand is the only man to get Adobe out of real trouble . . .

THE GUNMAN AND THE ACTRESS
Chap O'Keefe

To be paid a heap of money just for protecting a fancy French actress and her troupe of players didn't seem that difficult — but Joshua Dillard hadn't banked on the charms of the actress, and the fact that someone didn't want him even to reach the town . . .

HE RODE WITH QUANTRILL
Terry Murphy

Following the break-up of Quantrill's Raiders, both Jesse James and Mel Becher head their own gang. A decade later, their paths cross again when, unknowingly, they plan to rob the same bank — leading to a violent confrontation between Becher and James.

THE CLOVERLEAF CATTLE COMPANY
Lauran Paine

Bessie Thomas believed in miracles, and her husband, Jawn Henry, did not. But after finding a murdered settler and his woman, and running down the renegades responsible, Jawn Henry would have time to reflect. He and Bessie had never had children. Miracles evidently did happen.

COOGAN'S QUEST
J. P. Weston

Coogan came down from Wyoming on the trail of a man he had vowed to kill — Red Sheene, known as The Butcher. It was the kidnap of Marian De Quincey that gave Coogan his chance — but he was to need help from an unexpected quarter to avoid losing his own life.

DEATH COMES TO ROCK SPRINGS
Steven Gray

Jarrod Kilkline is in trouble with the army, the law, and a bounty hunter. Fleeing from capture, he rescues Brian Tyler, who has been left for dead by the three Jackson brothers. But when the Jacksons reappear on the scene, will Jarrod side with them or with the law in the final showdown?

GHOST TOWN
J. D. Kincaid

A snowstorm drove a motley collection of individuals to seek shelter in the ghost town of Silver Seam. When violence erupted, Kentuckian gunfighter Jack Stone needed all his deadly skills to secure his and an Indian girl's survival.

INCIDENT AT LAUGHING WATER CREEK
Harry Jay Thorn

All Kate Decker wants is to run her cattle along Laughing Water Creek. But Leland MacShane and Dave Winters want the whole valley to themselves, and they've hired an army of gunhawks to back their play. Then Frank Corcoran rides right into the middle of it . . .

THE BLUE-BELLY SERGEANT
Elliot Conway

After his discharge from the Union army, veteran Sergeant Harvey Kane hoped to settle down to a peaceful life. But when he took sides with a Texas cattle outfit in their fight against redlegs and reb-haters, he found that his killing days were far from over.

BLACK CANYON
Frank Scarman

All those who had robbed the train between Warbeck and Gaspard were now dead, including Jack Chandler, believed to be the only one who had known where the money was hidden. But someone else did know, and now, years later, waited for the chance to lift it . . .

LOWRY'S REVENGE
Ron Watkins

Frank Lowry's chances of avenging the murder of his wife by Sol Wesley are slim indeed. Frank has never fired a Colt revolver in anger, and he is up against the powerful Wesley family . . .

THE BLACK MARSHAL
John Dyson

Six-guns blazing, The Black Marshal rides into the Indian Nations intent upon imposing some law and order after his own family has been killed by desperadoes. Who can he trust? Only Judge Colt can decide.

KILLER'S HARVEST
Vic J. Hanson

A money man and a law deputy were murdered and a girl taken hostage by four badmen who went on the run. But they failed to reckon on veteran gunfighter Jay Lessiter, or on Goldie Santono's bandidos.

GUN-TOTING DRIFTER
Al Joyson

When John Gelder's ranch foreman is murdered, and Gelder is later forced to flee his own ranch, Deputy Sheriff Ben Winters is convinced that the new foreman, Jason Kenricks, holds the key to the mystery. But who is behind Kendricks? And why?

THE LAST RIDE
John Hunt

When horses were taken from the stage company's corralyard during a night raid. Cody Southwood, the town's sheriff, rounded up some townsmen and went after the thieves. They were to learn that people aren't always what they seem — and that a man's best friend is a loaded gun.